THE SEA CH

The Sea Change

& Other Stories

by

Helen Grant

Swan River Press
Dublin, Ireland
MMXXII

The Sea Change
by Helen Grant

Published by
Swan River Press
Dublin, Ireland
in February MMXXII

www.swanriverpress.ie
brian@swanriverpress.ie

Cover design by Meggan Kehrli
from artwork by Jason Zerrillo
based on a photograph by Iona Grant

Set in Garamond by Steve J. Shaw

Paperback Edition
ISBN 978-1-78380-758-1

Swan River Press published
a limited hardback edition of
The Sea Change in February 2013.

Contents

For Ben

Grauer Hans

"*Grauer Hans, geh weg von mir.*" That's all I can remember of the song. "Grey Hans, go away from me." There was a lot more of it, at least four verses, sung in my mother's rich contralto voice; I listened to it every night as far back as I can remember, up until the time we moved to England. I can't remember a time during my childhood when she didn't sing me to sleep with that song; she must have sung it to me the day I was born. I have the tune very well, but the memory of the words has somehow eroded away during the years, just as life has weathered me, blunting my youthful exuberance. All that remains now are those six words, "*Grauer Hans, geh weg von mir.*" I pray they are enough.

I was born at home, an occurrence that was already becoming rare at that time. My mother had an instinctive distrust of hospitals. Were she still alive today, she would be one of the many thousands of Germans who put their faith in homeopathy, herbal medicine, traditional remedies. The house stood on the cobbled main street of our home town; it was a traditional building made in the black-and-white half-timbered style, very common in the German Eifel; the rooms were long and low and the windows small; you would have thought there was a tax on daylight, so stingy an amount had the builders allowed in. I slept in a wooden cradle at the end of my mother's bed for the first year of my life; after that I had my own

3

little bedroom under the eaves, and it is there that I first remember her singing me the song about Grauer Hans. That is in fact my earliest memory: lying in my carved oak bed, which had been handed down from someone far back in my mother's side of the family, watching the coloured shapes from the revolving nightlight on my bedside table slithering across the low beams of the ceiling, and listening to my mother singing. "Grey Hans, go away from me." When I was very young there didn't seem anything strange about the song; in fact it was comforting, part of the nightly bedtime routine. No matter how tired she was, no matter how much work my mother had to do, she always sang right to the very end of the song. Then she would kiss me, run a hand through my hair in a wistful sort of way, and go downstairs.

I used to enjoy the bedtime routine; the warmth of my down quilt, the soft movement of the coloured lights, the sweet singing. And the visitor. He didn't come every night, but he came often enough that he became a kind of friend. I have always been a homebody, the sort of person who positively enjoys sitting inside a warm well-lit house watching the weather raging outside, warming my toes at the fire whilst rain and wind lash the windows. The visitor gave me that same sort of luxuriant feeling; I would lie in bed, the cover pulled up to my chin and my face turned to the little window, and watch for his face to come slyly peeping in. Sometimes it would be his twinkling eyes that I would see first; at other time the flash of white teeth would draw my eye. And there he would be, smiling in at me, a little apple-cheeked old man with bushy brows and a shock of hair the colour of newly-fallen snow. He could have been a kobold or a gnome, except that he never seemed to wear the green you might have expected; all his clothes, as far as I could make out through the little window panes, were a soft pearly colour which almost glowed against the dark background of the night sky. He would smile at me, and sometimes he would seem to laugh, although the sound was imperceptible through the glass. At other times he would paw or tap at the window, or make little signs to indicate that I should open the latch. But somehow the will to do so never came upon me; instead I would smile shyly back until sleep overcame me at last. It never worried me that the window was so high above the street, my room being on the third storey of the house; I never wondered how he got there, or how he got away again afterwards. If I thought about it at all, I must have concluded that he scurried across the rooftops like Saint Nicholas, peeping in at the windows of all the good little girls and boys.

I remember once, when I was about eight years old, I asked my mother about the bedtime song, about Grauer Hans. Why did she sing me that one every night? I wanted to know. My mother looked at me with an uneasy expression on her face. Did I want her to sing me another one as well as that one, she asked. I shook my head. What about *instead* of that one, I persisted? I didn't really care about having a new song; in fact I should have been sorry to change our nightly routine. But I was being perverse, as children will be. My mother hesitated. Then she said in a firm voice that the Grauer Hans song was traditional; she didn't see why she had to sing anything else, but if I really insisted she would sing me another one as well as "Grauer Hans". I looked at her, saw steel in her grey eyes, and simply shrugged. It was not that important to me.

I remembered that conversation a year or so later when my cousin Thilo came to stay. Thilo was fourteen, an unpromising age, and he was even less gracious than teenage boys of that age normally are, as his mother (my mother's sister) was seriously ill; perhaps the stress that Thilo was under made him more than usually disposed to tease and frighten me. He had the little bedroom next to mine, and he must have heard my mother singing to me at bedtime, for one afternoon when we were alone in the sitting room, he flicking through a magazine and I sketching out some design full of princesses and mythical animals, he suddenly said, "Does your mother always sing you that song?"

"What song?" I wanted to know.

"At bedtime," Thilo said impatiently. "You know, the one about Grauer Hans."

"Ye-e-s," I said doubtfully, expecting some sort of trap. Thilo had already in one short week proved himself an adept at getting me to say stupid things and make a fool of myself.

"Hah, you baby," he sneered.

As he had anticipated, I bristled. "I don't want the silly song," I told him mendaciously. "I told her to stop singing it ages ago, but she wanted to go on with it. She says it's traditional."

"So it's Aunt Christa who—" and here Thilo used a German expression which literally means that someone has one too many rafters, but which is like saying they have bats in the belfry in English. Of course I flew at him then, and there was such a rumpus that my mother came in and told us both to shut up. She had been trying to telephone her brother-in-law, Thilo's father, for news, otherwise she might have asked us about the source of the fight, but in the event she left us with several dire threats if we disturbed her once more, and went off again.

After she had gone, Thilo and I glared at each other for several moments in silence. Then Thilo said in a wheedling voice, "Haven't you ever wondered why she sings you that song every night, then?"

"I told you, it's traditional," I said stolidly.

He regarded me with a malicious glint in his eyes. "I bet you don't even know who Grauer Hans is."

I picked up my pencils again and pretended to study the crumpled picture I had abandoned when I went for him. I said nothing.

"Don't you want to know?" he persisted, and when he got no response: "I bet she thinks you'd be too scared."

I lifted my head and looked into his cold blue eyes with what I hoped was an air of nonchalance. "Scared of what?"

"Of Grauer Hans, of course."

"It's just a song," I said—and indeed, up to that moment, it had never occurred to me to think of Grauer Hans as anything other than a line in a song; I hadn't thought of him as a *person*. Now it appeared that not only was he a person, but he was someone *frightening*. Grauer Hans, it was Thilo's delight to inform me, was a bogey, a monster, a demon. A leprous grey all over, he could slide invisibly through the night shadows, slither unseen through the camouflaging masses of cobwebs under the eaves, and tap at the window of his intended victim with his misshapen fingers, the claws scratching the glass like diamonds. His victim was always a child. He had evil little red eyes which gleamed dully like blood blisters, and he had no nose, only a long triangular hole, and he had a great prognathous jaw which he could unhook like a snake's to reveal a double row of gleaming teeth like skinning knives. Let him once get in at the window and he would carry his prize away over the rooftops, screaming and thrashing. What happened to them afterwards no-one knew, but none of them was ever seen again . . .

Thilo's revelation made me sick with horror. I think I went very pale, for he smiled maliciously. I wrapped my arms around myself, as though to keep myself safe. "I don't believe you," I said, tremblingly. "Why would my mother sing me a song about something so horrible as that?"

"Why, to keep him off, stupid," said Thilo.

It was a wonder really, that I went to bed that night and submitted to lying there on my own in my little dark room under the eaves, without having a massive fit of the hysterics. When my mother sang the song, I turned my face away from her and tried to concentrate on the shifting shapes from the coloured lantern as they swam and dissolved across the beams. When she went downstairs I huddled under the quilt, not daring to look out, not daring to look at the window. After what seemed a long time, I thought I heard something, a very faint scratching or rubbing at the glass, and with fearful reluctance I peered out from under my nest of covers. But no monstrous visage was peering in at me through the little panes; only the familiar apple-cheeked face of my night-time visitor, his dark eyes twinkling like a bird's. He beamed at me, drumming his fingers on the glass, and I smiled back at him, and fell asleep at last, reassured.

Well, time passed; Thilo's mother recovered, much to everyone's surprise and relief, and Thilo went back to his parents. He never mentioned Grauer Hans to me again, and our parting was fairly amicable, but all the same his revelation had left its mark on me. I was a suggestible child—perhaps it came from being on my own too much, for I had no siblings, and my mother being a lone parent was obliged to work, and left me to myself a great deal—and I fretted. The bedtime song no longer seemed reassuring; rather, it was a cause for a concern which was showing signs of becoming obsessive. What would happen if my mother failed to sing all of the verses one night? Or if she neglected to sing it altogether? I would lie there whilst she

sang, fearfully listening for omissions or even mistakes—
for who knew what slight deviation from the proper
words or tune might render the protective properties of
the song invalid? After she had gone, and I had heard the
last stair creak under her departing footsteps, I would lie
there wretchedly in the dark, wondering if Grauer Hans
would come tapping on my window. Even the visits of
my jolly little nocturnal friend failed to comfort me; I
fancied now that I saw a new expression in his eyes—a
little sadness, a little disappointment. Perhaps he could see
how the child in the carved oak bed was growing thin and
pale with worry. I hardly cared to meet his eyes any more.
Once, when I did, I fancied I saw more than reproach in
them; I thought I saw irritation, the beginning of anger.
And perhaps it was my depressed state of mind, or perhaps
it was the departing glamour of youth, but I fancied his
pearly suit had begun to look a little dingy, a little drab.

At length my mother, busy and preoccupied as she
was, noticed that her only daughter was growing drawn
with worry, that I had dark rings under my eyes from the
long nights when I had hardly dared to close my eyes.
Disregarding my wan protestations that nothing was
wrong, she determined to have a serious talk with me;
she made me a little mug of *Kindertee*, children's fruit tea
flavoured with raspberry and vanilla with a liberal teaspoon
of sugar in it, she sat down with me at the kitchen table
and earnestly begged me to tell her what the matter was.
At first I said nothing, feeling very acutely how ridiculous
it was that a great girl of nearly ten was worrying about a
story meant to frighten babies; also I had a vague feeling
that putting my fears into words would somehow make
things worse. But in the end, of course, it all came out:
what Thilo had said about Grauer Hans, and my worrying
about the song, whether she would forget a bit or make

a mistake; whether I would wake up one night and see Grauer Hans's glowing red eyes on the other side of the glass . . .

I expected my mother to comfort me, to hug me close and tell me that it was all a lot of superstitious nonsense, that there was no real Grauer Hans—perhaps even that Thilo himself had made up all the stuff about the glowing red eyes and the teeth like skinning knives. I thought perhaps she would laugh. But she didn't; instead she became very thoughtful, gazing at the tabletop where she rubbed her finger in the wet ring mark where my cup had been. Then she told me very quietly that she would never, *ever*, forget to sing the song, nor would she leave a single word of it out. If she made a mistake, she would sing it again from the beginning if I liked. I was not to worry. If she intended to comfort me by this, her words had the opposite effect. I didn't like the grave look on her face; an older person might have assumed she was trying to make me feel that she was taking my fears seriously, but to me, a child, it meant that she was afraid too. I refused to leave the matter there. I asked other questions; I wanted to know whether it was true about the leprous grey colour, about the hole for a nose. What did Grauer Hans do with you once he had carried you off? Was it true that none of his victims had ever been seen again? Did she personally know of anyone—any child—who had been taken away by Grauer Hans? And how did they know it was him?

So many questions, and they all bounced off like a handful of gravel flung against a window pane. My mother was reluctant to discuss the details of Grauer Hans and what he was supposed to do to his victims; at first all that she would say was that I was not to be afraid, and that she would sing me the song every night, right through to the end. To the question about whether she knew anyone who

10

had been taken away by Grauer Hans, she simply pursed her lips tightly and shook her head. But finally, after a good deal of pleading and nagging on my behalf, she told me that, yes, Grauer Hans was supposed to be grey all over (how else would he have come by his name?) and to have a great many teeth, though she told me this simply and matter-of-factly, omitting any comparison to skinning knives and the like. I think she wished to avoid frightening me any more than I already was, but in fact her dispassionate description was somehow worse than Thilo's gothic one. Of course it ended with my bursting into hysterical tears and clinging to my mother as though Grauer Hans himself were about to prise me away from her.

My mother let me cry for a few minutes, stroking my hair with her hand as though trying to soothe a frightened animal. Then at last, when my sobs had degenerated into hiccups and I was able to sit up and wipe my eyes with the back of my hand, she took me by the shoulders and told me to look at her. I did so, sniffing wetly and trying to brush back the strands of hair which had stuck to my tear-damp face. Then my mother told me that I need not fear seeing the glowing red eyes, the hole-for-a-nose and the wickedly-sharp teeth of Grauer Hans; for Grauer Hans never appeared in that form to a child. Here she checked herself, and said that he was never *supposed* to appear in that form, trying unsuccessfully to maintain the idea that we were chatting through the details of a quaint old folktale. Only the very rare and unlucky adult who glimpsed him would see his true form, that was what *they*—other people—said; before puberty (I had only a vague idea what she meant by that) he would appear in an attractive form, one designed to charm rather than frighten. After all, was the unspoken implication, why would anyone open the window to a monster?

11

How did he look to children, then? I wanted to know. My mother smiled at me a little nervously. Oh, she said, offhandedly, he sometimes appeared as a fairy, with a fluff of flaxen hair and bright eyes like a bird's, and clothes all over spangles; and sometimes he appeared like a little old man, something like a gnome, with apple cheeks and bushy eyebrows . . .

"You mean like . . . ?" I started to say, and stopped short, shocked at my own words. For a moment there was silence between us, as my mother stared at me, an expression of horror curdling on her features.

"Like *what?*" she shrieked, seizing me by the upper arms and shaking me until my teeth chattered. Suddenly she let go and we stared at each other, panting.

"Like what?" she said again, but this time her voice was almost a whisper, as though she hardly dared ask the question, nor hear the answer.

"Like . . . like the visitor . . . " I stammered, feeling as though I had done something terribly wrong, but not sure why. "The one who taps on my window at night-time, when you've gone downstairs . . . "

Then it all came out. The many nights when I had lain in my bed, snuggled tight under the covers, my face turned to the window, to see my little friend, his beaming face pressed close to the panes, pawing at the glass with his fingers. How I had looked forward to seeing him; how friendly he seemed, with his rosy-red cheeks and his bushy white brows, his eyes twinkling like a bird's. How he had signed and signed for me to open the latch and let him in, but how I had never managed to summon up the energy to get out of bed and do it, lulled as I was by my mother's song . . . the song about Grauer Hans. How I had grown fearful at night-time, and hardly even dared look out for my little friend any more, and how it seemed to me that

12

his expression had grown less genial as a result; first he had looked sad, and sometimes now he even seemed angry . . .

"Even his clothes don't look so nice anymore," I said ingenuously. "They used to look all shiny, like pearls, but now they're starting to look . . . "

"Grey," finished my mother. Her voice was brittle and distant, as though she were forcing herself to skim across the surface of some great emotion, instead of plunging into it. "He's not angry with you," she went on. "You're growing older. You're starting to see him . . . " Abruptly she broke off. There was a short silence, and then my mother got to her feet.

"Where are you going?" I asked her.

She looked at me. "You can help. Come on, I'm moving your bed into my room."

I must have shared my mother's room for nearly a year, my little bed squeezed into the corner furthest from the window. But I don't really remember how it was, whether it felt strange lying there amongst her things, the dressing-table covered with bottles and jars, the old pink bathrobe hanging on the back of the door, the lamp with its golden shade. Whether I fell asleep before my mother came up to bed. Whether my mother snored, or talked in her sleep. The only thing which stands out in my mind from that time is one night—one particular night. I think it was October; the last warmth of the Indian summers we so often experienced in the Eifel had gone, and the nights were crisp, clear and cold. I had stayed up late finishing a piece of work for school the next morning, and had gone to my bed in my mother's room feeling tired and worn. I must have fallen asleep almost as soon as my head touched the pillow, but my slumber was uneasy. I had the most curious dream. It seemed to me that whilst I was lying there, I heard someone calling me, but I could not tell you what words they used; all I retained was the impression of urgency, a shapeless insistence, like a fish-hook snagging in my deepest consciousness. I dreamed I arose from my bed as silently as I could, and weaved my way around the furniture which divided me from the door, as though my mother had purposely laid obstacles in my way. In my dream I set my bare feet upon the wooden staircase and climbed it slowly and carefully, so that the treads would not creak under me. It was a curious dream, indeed, for in it I could see the light which came from the sitting-room downstairs, and the nagging sound of my mother's sewing-machine as it raced across the fabric of a new dress. It was marvellously realistic. I dreamed I went to the door of my old room and pushed it gently so that it swung silently open, revealing the denuded spaces within, silvered by moonlight. Into the room I glided in my dream, my thin nightdress a poor protection against the chill. Someone was waiting for me on the other side of the familiar little window; my visitor. I dreamed I saw him smiling at me, his little bird-eyes twinkling with recognition, his bunched cheeks rosy-red; it was like greeting a long-lost friend. With eager feet I pattered to the window, with trembling fingers I worked at the stiff catch. How strange, to feel the cold metal under one's touch, even in a dream! How strange, too, to look through glass which seemed to run and distort like water, so that the figure on the other side seemed to run too, like candlewax, the black eyes streaming red, the pearly clothes rippling into grey. I should have stopped then, I should have run downstairs as fast as my bare feet could carry me, calling for my mother; but in a dream our will is not always our own. My fingers still worked at the latch, which was beginning to come free. At last it popped open, bruising my fingers, and the window opened a crack, admitting a little steam which might have been breath hanging on the cold night air. There was a faint feral odour, the whiff of some carrion feeder's lair. On the outside window-sill claws were scratching and skittering; two eyes glowed redly in the darkness. In the dream I had knowledge that was denied to my waking hours; I knew I must open the window myself; that he could not come in unless I did so. Very deliberately I grasped the latch and began to open the window. And now the dream became a nightmare; for what was this mummy's hand—this sickeningly-sharp bundle of talons, the grey skin stretched tightly over sinews like steel hawsers—this hand which clutched the window frame, seeking a purchase? A scream curdled in my throat, for now I saw him clearly: Grauer Hans, crouched on my window-sill like some gigantic pterodactyl, his bunched limbs almost filling the window frame. He was everything Thilo had told me, and worse; who could have imagined the sickening madness of those glaring crimson eyes, the obscenity of a face, with a gaping triangular hole at its concave centre and a disproportionate jaw, which sagged open to reveal teeth like those of a white shark, jagged and savage? With sick horror I gazed at a tiny string of saliva which hung between the jaws, glistening silver in the moonlight. Grauer Hans meant to champ and grind my tender flesh between those cleaver-like fangs of his, and in the paralysis of my dream I could not even turn my white face away from him.

I do not think I screamed, even then; but suddenly the air was rent with the eldritch shrieking of a berserker. My mother was in the room with me, screaming as though she would burst her lungs, and beating at something with the violence of a lunatic. I saw she had the thick poker from the kitchen and was wielding it like a club; the crash of the metal on the window frame and walls and—something else—sounded like a series of explosions to me; they seemed to shatter me, to shiver my consciousness into a thousand pieces like a broken mirror. I trembled; I closed my eyes, and clenched my hands into fists. But I could not shut out the sounds which permeated through all the rumpus; the snarling, the furious howling of a carnivorous beast despoiled of its prey. When the window was finally jammed shut and my mother was fastening the latch with hands that shook as though she had a palsy, it was as though she were shutting out a storm, a storm which still lashed at the panes with frustrated force and rattled the window in its frame.

A dream, it was a dream . . . I opened my eyes at last and my mother was there, leaning against the wall and panting, her hair over her eyes, her cheeks red with exertion. For a long moment we stared at each other without speaking.

"Mama?" My voice felt like cotton wool, my throat was thick and dry. "Mama, am I dreaming?"

"Yes," she said. "Yes, my child, yes, yes." She reached for me with trembling hands. "Come to bed," she said. "Come back to bed."

That was when I was nine, nearly ten years old. By the time I was eleven we had left that house, left the town, left Germany altogether. My mother, who was still a young and handsome woman, met my stepfather, an Englishman from Birmingham who was living in the area for a few months on some sort of business secondment. When they married within the year, and we all moved back to England, everyone said it was a whirlwind romance; it must be true love, they said, for my mother to take up with him so fast and leave the town where she and her family had always lived. I thought otherwise, and still do: my stepfather was not an unpleasant man—he was ordinary and kind—but my mother mainly saw him as a means of getting away. The day we packed up the last of our things in the little low house on the high street, I saw her go to the window of my bedroom and rattle the handle sharply, as though testing the latch. Then she saw me looking at her, shrugged with fierce disregard and stalked past me out of the room. I did not see the house again for years; instead we exchanged the rolling green fields and dark swathes of pine forest of the Eifel for the wet pavements and grey streets of Birmingham.

After fifteen years in England I was almost English; indeed my German acquaintances, such as they are, tell me that I now speak German with a faint English accent. I finished my schooling there and started work; I didn't make it to university, but I didn't regret it until later, when I had two of us to support. My stepfather died at fifty-five of a heart attack, leaving my mother with enough to live on, but only just. Meanwhile I met someone and played out the tired old story; he had a wife already, but she didn't understand him like I did; I gave myself to him, got pregnant, and then watched him run a mile. I moved back in with my mother, now bitterly regretting the fact that I was only qualified to do the sort of job that does not come with generous maternity pay and all sorts of exciting job-sharing options for the new mother. We managed for a while, though it was becoming clear that our ship was sinking; as fast as we baled out our debts, more came flooding in. Then my mother, my much-loved mother, who had been born Christa Nettersheim in the German Eifel and had become Christa Roberts in Birmingham, England, to save me, suddenly died of an aneurism. Amidst my grief came the ever more pressing issue of how I should live; the income my mother had had from my stepfather had died with her. It was then that I discovered that my mother had left me the house. Not the house in Birmingham—that had to be sold, as it was mortgaged up to the hilt—but the one in Germany, in the town where I was born.

And that is how I came to be here again, living in the very house where I was born.

My mother has gone, my stepfather has gone, even my irritating cousin Thilo has gone, killed in a road accident three years after we left Germany. It's just me—and my daughter Marla. She's a beautiful child, with blue eyes the colour of the *Kornblume*, the cornflower, and golden hair which clusters in soft curls all over her little head. She is all I have, all I shall ever have (since I have no desire to take up with another man). I love her to distraction. And oh, how I fear for her.

She's ten months old now. Old enough to sit up, but not old enough to crawl yet. But in a few months she *will* crawl, and in a year's time she will be walking. She will be old enough by then to toddle around the house, to pick things up, to explore; perhaps she will already be able to climb out of her cot on her own, to make her own way across the room on her unsteady little legs; perhaps she will be able to climb up stairs, climb onto the furniture, anything to enable her to reach a little higher. Her little hands, which can already grip her rattle and her stuffed bunny with surprising strength, will be able to grasp things firmly— things like handles, knobs—and window latches. If she saw something outside her window late at night, when I have fallen into a dire and dream-racked slumber, she might be able to get up all by herself, to climb onto a chair, to reach up . . . it is at this point that imagination reaches the end of the trail, the mind flinches back. It *must not* be so.

I have tried to remember the song; I heard it every night for eleven years, of course. But I lived so long in England that I almost became English, and I forgot the words—all except that last line: "*Grauer Hans, geh weg von mir*". I sing them over and over again, praying that it will be enough. And every night when Marla is in her cot, I go around the whole house, every floor, every room, checking the locks and bolts, making sure everything is secure. I rattle the little window in her room, checking that the latch is firmly done up, that there is not even one millimetre's movement of the window in its frame, not even space for an ant to crawl through. Later, when I make up my bed on the floor of her room, I deliberately turn my face away from that window and ignore the sounds which begin stealthily, but grow bolder when the light is out and the hours grow later. The thin scratching as though someone is drawing a diamond across the glass. The faint rattling of someone pawing at the panes. Mostly Marla sleeps through it all, but once I saw her wake up and turn her little face to the window. Whatever she saw, she was not afraid; she beamed at it with the cherubic smile she usually reserves for me. But I am afraid; I am afraid that if I looked I would see something which used to be dressed all in pearly white when I saw it as a child, something which is really grey all over, a phosphorescent, leprous grey. Something with eyes of a dull red, as though the orbs had filled up with blood. Something with a grinning jaw that sags open to reveal rows of teeth like skinning knives. Something called *Grauer Hans*.

The Sea Change

The thing you have to understand about Daffy is that he had a polite, but complete, lack of regard for Rules. Daffy was one of the most laid-back people I have ever met. He got up when he felt like it, he shaved if he felt like it, and he ambled along to appointments when he was ready. He parked on double yellow lines, he turned up to his own brother's wedding in jeans. And sometimes he liked to dive alone.

Maybe that last one doesn't strike you as being such a big deal. Maybe you've never learnt to dive, not even to five metres amongst the multi-coloured fish whilst on holiday in the Canaries. So maybe you're not aware that the absolute bedrock of any sports diving system, whether it's the British Sub-Aqua Club (traditionally hot on safety) or the Professional Association of Diving Instructors (not keen on losing anyone either), is buddy diving. Like newlyweds, you do everything in pairs. You kit up together, you check each other's gear, you hit the water together, you fin around on the bottom keeping each other in sight (using a buddy line if the conditions are really filthy, as they often are in British waters) and you both surface at the same time too. Then you sign each other's log books as a way of plighting your troth. Well, that's what most of us do. Not Daffy, though.

Daffy isn't his proper name, of course. He was christened Jonathan Edwin Duckett. But his name didn't really suit him—Jonathan sounds much too formal—and once some wit in the local pub had christened him Daffy Duckett, it just stuck. After all those years I doubt he'd have turned round if anyone had yelled "Jonathan!" in a crowded bar. Daffy it was. He was not a particularly tall man, but he was sturdy. He was carrying a bit of a belly too. You won't see that on marathon runners or squash players, but plenty of divers carry a bit of ballast at the front. Daffy used to say it helped keep him warm. He had blue eyes, cornflower blue, but faded, as though the salt water had taken all the colour out of them, and a mop of greying hair which was always sticking up every which way; I think it was permanently encrusted with salt. His skin was salt-roughened too, and when he smiled, which he did a lot, his face broke up into a thousand wrinkles, like tidal flats.

I met Daffy through a mutual love of diving. He had a dive boat, a battered looking thing moored in a little marina on the Dorset coast, and a dive shop, which he sometimes manned himself—the rest of the time it was run by an unending succession of put-upon temporary staff. He ran the shop and offered diving trips in order to fund his own passion for sub-aqua, which was limitless. Most of his custom was strictly seasonal—people who wanted to dive in summer sunshine on a calm sea and go and have a beer in a pub garden afterwards. Daffy himself went diving in all sorts of unpromising weather, starting earlier and ending later in the season than anyone else. I reckon if the sea had frozen over, he'd have sawn a hole in the ice and gone diving anyway. When he wasn't taking clients out, he had a group of cronies he used to dive with, all of them as salty-looking as himself. And sometimes he used to dive on his own.

"But Daffy," I said to him once, not long after we'd met: "Don't you worry about what might happen if you got into trouble?"

"No," he said, shaking his head and giving me that lazy grin of his.

"What if you get caught in some net?" I persisted.

"Got a net knife, haven't I?" he said. We were in that shop of his at the time, and he picked a knife up off the counter as if to illustrate the point. "You can have one too, if you like. A tenner, 'cause I know you."

"I've got two already." Daffy had sold me both of them—one for carrying on dives and a spare in case I lost the first one—as he well knew. I couldn't help laughing at his cheek though, and the subject of his solo diving was dropped for the time being. I'm mainly telling you about it because it was his established habit of diving alone that prevented me from being suspicious later on—but I'm getting ahead of myself now.

Daffy and I did quite a few dives together over a period of several years. His scrawl of a signature adorns a fair number of pages in my log book. I couldn't return the compliment because Daffy had stopped keeping a log of his dives after he'd done about six hundred of them. He said it was because he did all his dives in British water and he got fed up with writing, "Low viz; saw some kelp."

I might have given the impression from what I have told you about Daffy, that he was a dubious choice of diving buddy, unreliable and cavalier about safety. Nothing could be further from the truth. Apart from his habit of diving alone (which was his responsibility, after all), he was a very careful diver. I never saw him go into the water with less than a full tank, or come up without a respectable safety margin of air left in it. He always carried the ubiquitous net knife in case of entanglement, and he was always generous in the time he gave to decompression stops. He also had a very calm body language under water. You might not think there is such a thing, but there is.

Everything he did was relaxed and unhurried, but definite. It had quite a calming effect, even on the most nervous buddy. You could have put the greenest of novices in the water with Daffy and they'd have been as safe as houses in those weather-beaten hands.

That was really why I agreed to go out on the boat with him that May morning. Normally once you get into the beginning of May you're right into the diving season, but that year the weather had been filthy right through the spring. It's one thing to dive when the water's a bit chilly or there's a spring shower coming down, but if the sea is really rough—"lumpy", Daffy used to call it—you can forget it. Even if you managed to get into the water safely, whoever was manning the boat would never find you when you came up again, and even if they did, you certainly couldn't climb back up the ladder. So even Daffy had had a lean time of it so far that year, forced to content himself with a couple of inland dives in quarries and suchlike. Anyway, about two days before this particular trip, there had been the mother of all storms. It was one of those which makes it onto the national news, with cars being swept off the quayside and into the sea, and trees crashing through people's roofs. It was as if Mother Nature was having a major tantrum, and once she'd got it all out of her system she calmed down straight away.

The day after the storm dawned clear and fair, and at slack water the sea was like glass. I'd dropped into Daffy's shop to buy some spare o-rings and look at gloves (my old ones were getting past it); Daffy was behind the counter, the latest of his downtrodden assistants having handed in his notice, and he suggested a dive the following day if the weather held. The next day the weather was just as fabulously calm, and even becoming hot, so off we went. There were just the two of us diving, and Daffy had dug up a gormless looking youth in saggy jeans and a baseball cap to handle the boat whilst we were in the water. The gormless youth wasn't going to dive: you could see that at once from the red eyes and the streaming nose. I kept my distance; a head cold can keep you off diving for weeks.

The plan was to make the first dive onto a wreck at about twenty-three metres, one we had done several times in the past. Daffy had gone a lot deeper in the past, of course—listen to any group of divers in the pub and someone's sure to be bragging about "fifty metre bounce dives" and so forth—but as this was practically the first dive of the season we decided to be conservative. We thought we'd have some lunch on the boat afterwards, and then do a drift dive later in shallower water. We chugged out of the marina, and once the buildings on the shorefront had started to look like a row of dolls' houses, Daffy switched on the sonar. We were nowhere near the wreck yet, but when conversation failed or we got fed up looking at the horizon, we could amuse ourselves watching the contours of the sea-bed unravelling across the little screen. Sometimes an indefinite mass would move across the middle of the screen and that would be a shoal of fish. But mostly you would just see sea-bed unrolling as we went over it.

Eventually I got bored with the sonar and went out of the cabin to look over my diving kit. I was kneeling on the deck adjusting one of the straps on my dive knife when I heard Daffy say "Hello" in a puzzled voice. Then I felt the boat judder as he cut the engine.

"Okay?" I called, straightening up. I went back into the cabin. "What's up? Did we overshoot?"

"Overshoot? No," said Daffy, still sounding nonplussed. "We're nowhere near the dive site yet. It's just . . . look." He was pointing to the sonar screen. I looked, but couldn't see anything out of the ordinary. I shrugged. "Can't see anything."

"Damn it, we've passed over it," said Daffy. "Hold on, I'm going to turn round and go back over it." He started up again, and we did as tight a turn as that old tub of his could manage, getting a lungful of foul-tasting fumes from the engine in the process. Then we chugged along slowly, back in the direction we had come from. Both of us watched the screen. Then suddenly Daffy said, "There." I looked at the screen, and sure enough there was something underneath us. It was a definite hump or mound on the sea bottom, just over twenty metres down, and it was fairly big. It was difficult to tell just how big from the sonar but it wasn't a cluster of old lobster pots, I'm telling you that. Still, I couldn't see why Daffy was getting so excited about it.

"Is it a wreck, do you think?" I hazarded.

He shook his head. "I've never been over one around here before."

I didn't say anything to this; Daffy's knowledge of those waters and their more interesting features was encyclopaedic, but I didn't see how even he could claim to know every single wreck in that stretch of sea-bed.

Eventually I said, "A reef?"

"Not unless it's sprung up overnight," he said drily. "Gavin?" He called the gormless youth over and told him to take over whilst we kitted up.

"We're going in? Here?" I asked, following Daffy out of the cabin.

"Yep," he said, hefting his weight belt in one hand.

"What about the *Callisto*?" I said, referring to the wreck we had planned to dive.

"She'll keep," said Daffy. Now he'd got the belt done up and was making a last check of his air, turning it on and off and watching the pressure gauge. He shot me a glance with those faded blue eyes. "Come on, woman—where's your sense of adventure?"

I held up my hands. "All right—I just hope whatever it is is worth seeing."

Five minutes later we hit the water. Gormless Gavin hoisted the A-flag to indicate that there were divers down. Daffy gave the thumbs-down signal and we started to let the air out of our jackets. The water closed over our heads and the sounds of sea-birds and the boat's engine were replaced by the bubbling of air escaping as we exhaled.

It's a funny thing, but although I've done over a hundred dives, and about half of them have been on wrecks, there's still something about descending onto one that gives me the heeby-jeebies. Diving in British waters is not like diving in Egypt, or in the Canary Islands, where it's like being in a tropical fish-tank, everything a lovely shade of blue and crystal clear. No; in British waters you can expect a sort of endless greeny-grey murk that sometimes degenerates into the aquatic version of a pea-souper. You can't study a wrecked ship from a great height as you slowly and gracefully descend towards it; more likely you will keep sinking further and further into the murk and then suddenly you will find you are sitting on it. It always gives me the willies, that moment when you see some spar or piece of rusting metalwork looming up at you out of the gloom.

Anyway, down we went, and reading my depth gauge I saw we had passed eighteen metres and should be at the bottom any minute now. Then it materialised underneath me, as though a blurred photograph had suddenly come into focus, and I found myself coming down onto the seabed, a grey surface of sand and stones. Daffy was next to me, vigorously clearing his ears. We gave each other the okay sign, and then we looked about us. The visibility wasn't great—a lot of muck had evidently been stirred up by the recent storm—but almost at once I saw what looked like a couple of spars or posts sticking up from the sea-bed. Daffy had evidently seen them too, as he indicated ahead with one hand and we finned forward to take a closer look. It was difficult to tell quite what we were looking at; whatever it was, it had either been down there a very long time indeed or it had been pretty badly smashed up. The posts—or whatever they were—were of wood, blackened and softened by long exposure to the salt water. By the lack of weed or other adhesions such as barnacles I should say that they had lain under a covering of sand and stones until the turbulence of the recent storm had uncovered them. But that's only a guess, of course. I touched one tentatively, my hands blue-grey and ghostly in the light filtered down through the water above us. There was very little movement in it; evidently it was still firmly attached to some other beam or timber below the level of the sea-bed.

Whilst I was examining it, Daffy touched my arm, and when I turned my head he pointed. Dimly visible in the green-grey murk was another of the posts, and yet another one beyond it, if I strained my eyes. We finned towards them, and as we drew closer, we could make out more of them, gradually looming into focus. I had the impression that the line was slightly curved, although it was difficult to tell; perspective does funny things under water.

Well, we finned along the line, looking out for anything a little more distinctive to tell us what we were looking at; so far the wreck or whatever it was seemed too badly broken up to be recognisable. Frankly, I was surprised that it had appeared to be so extensive and so large on the sonar, as there was not much to see other than the posts or spars, and they only protruded, I should say, about four feet from the sea-bed at most. Abruptly we came to the end of the line and discovered that it turned back on itself, creating a kind of acute angle which might have represented the bows of a craft, though there was nothing to distinguish it, no bowsprit or anything like that. The line of posts receded away into the gloom, mirroring the line we had just followed. For the first time, I began to map the site in my mind's eye. Clearly it formed something like an ellipse, the posts or spars sticking up like the teeth of an open trap . . . and we had landed right dead centre in the middle of it.

Somehow I didn't like that idea. Nor did I much fancy staying there. Call me superstitious if you like, but I reckon most divers have times and places when they know it isn't right—you're not meant to be in the water that day. And on top of that—well, I had a peculiar sensation of being watched. I know how barmy that sounds. There's nothing down at twenty metres to watch you unless you count the fish, right? All the same, I had this feeling . . . so I tapped Daffy on the arm and indicated that we should swim directly across the nearest line of posts, and out. He looked at me, his eyes unreadable behind his mask, then held up one hand. *Hold on a minute*, he was saying. Then he indicated that we should continue to swim along the line, and without waiting for me to confirm, he finned off. Now I was not so much uneasy as rather irritated. I finned along behind him as he skimmed past the line of posts, the fluorescent yellow tips of his fins seeming to flash in the murky water.

As I swam, I reached for my contents gauge, pulled it towards me, and checked my air. I was surprised to see that two-thirds of it had been consumed already. It was my first dive of the season, yes, but I didn't think I was as unfit as all that. Nor was I aware that I had been breathing particularly quickly. When Daffy stopped to examine another of the posts, I tapped his arm, and pointed to the gauge. I held up one hand, the fingers splayed, then jerked a thumb upwards. *Five minutes. Then up.* I wondered for a moment whether he had understood; then he signed back, pointing at me and then jabbing his own thumb upwards. *You go up.* He paused, then pointed at his own chest and then at the sea bed. *I'm staying here.* I found myself shaking my head, which was useless of course. Then I reached out and took his wrist very firmly in my hand. I pointed at him, then at myself, then made the thumb movement again. *We are both going up.* He could dive on his own without me if he liked, but I wasn't leaving a buddy halfway through a dive. Daffy pulled his arm away with a gesture of irritation, but the message had got through. He made the *up* sign and immediately started to let air into his stab jacket. I fumbled with my own air feed, then followed him upwards, watching the staccato movements of his fins; I could tell he was mad.

He didn't speak to me whilst we were waiting for Gormless Gavin to pick us up. Once we were back on the boat he began methodically to take his diving kit off, engrossing himself in the routine. He turned off the air and laid the bottle on its side. He unclipped his weight belt and put it neatly out of the way where no-one would stub a toe on it. All the time he failed to catch my eye. For myself—well, I was a little irritated too. What else was I supposed to have done? I wasn't going to stay down there until I ran out of air, nor was I going to abandon a buddy on a dive. I decided to leave him until he snapped out of it—which he eventually did. Gavin broke out the sandwiches (which I took rather gingerly, praying he had not sneezed all over them) and passed round hot black coffee from a flask. Daffy took an enormous swig of coffee, smacked his lips, then gave me a broad grin.

"You need a bigger bottle," he informed me.

I shook my head, smiling. "Got too many in stock?" I asked.

"I'll do you a deal."

"I should have left you down there," I replied, laughing.

We parted late in the afternoon and I didn't see Daffy for a few days after that. I dropped by the dive shop one lunchtime, but Gavin was behind the till, flicking aimlessly through a diving magazine. He did not look as though he had the energy or drive to attempt any of the spectacular dives featured, nor did he look ready to be engaged in one of those long conversations about equipment which divers love to have. In the end I left without buying anything.

A week later I went down to the marina late in the afternoon and found Daffy and Gavin unloading gear from the boat. I stood on the jetty with my hand over my eyes to keep out the glare of the sun, and watched them lifting equipment out. I noticed there was only one bottle, only one stab jacket, dripping water onto the salt-bleached boards.

"Been diving?" I said, stating the obvious.

"Yep," said Daffy succinctly, retrieving a fin from the bottom of the boat.

"Customers?" I said.

"No, just us," said Daffy.

"Who did the boat handling, then?" I asked.

"Gavin." Daffy cocked his head to one side and looked up at me with one eye screwed up, as though trying to ascertain my point.

"Who did you dive with, then?" I persisted.

"Me, myself and I," said Daffy with cheerful unconcern.

"Daffy . . . " I couldn't keep the reproach out of my tone.

"Catch," he said by way of reply, lobbing a mask and snorkel at me. Then he climbed out of the boat and stood in front of me on the jetty. I shook my head at him.

"One of these days . . . " I said warningly.

" . . . I'll die of thirst," he finished. "Come on, are we going to the pub or what?"

That was in May. I didn't dive much for some weeks after that; I had caught Gavin's horrible cold, and even after the worst of it had gone, my ears felt as though they were gummed up with superglue. I did a shallow shore dive with my club—or tried to—but my ears resolutely refused to clear. There was no question of attempting anything deeper without the risk of real damage. I used every nasal spray and decongestant I could lay hands on, and I sulked. Once or twice I went down to the marina to see if Daffy were about. The first time his boat had gone. The second time it was there, but Daffy was nowhere to be seen. Gavin was securing the boat on his own. I greeted him, and he eventually returned the greeting, though reluctantly; I'm not sure if he was in an unfriendly mood or was simply too dim to recognise me.

"Been out diving?" I asked.

He nodded.

I peered into the boat and could see no gear lying around. Clearly Daffy had been able to carry all of it with him. He must have been diving alone again, I surmised.

"Daffy been in on his own again?" I asked, sticking my neck out.

He looked at me for a moment, then made a slight flicking gesture with his head. It might have been a yes or a no. I nodded at him, unwilling to waste any more words on this taciturn lump, and left him to it.

I ran Daffy to earth in his favourite corner of the pub across the road from the marina. He was sitting hunched over a pint of bitter, his hands jammed into his armpits and his shoulders almost at his ears, as though he were freezing cold. He looked ill. His face had a greyish tinge to it, as though he had been chilled to the point of hypothermia. The pint seemed to be untasted. I slid into the seat opposite him and he looked up and gave me a smile. It was a real Daffy grin, and seemed to transform him at once; in fact a little colour came back into his cheeks.

"Still full of cold, you jessie?" was his friendly greeting.

I snorted. "I bet I don't look as bad as you do. Where have you been diving today—Antarctica?"

He shrugged, as if to show that it was of little importance. "That wreck at twenty metres," he said.

"The one we did together?" I was incredulous. "What for? There was nothing to see."

"Ah," said Daffy mysteriously. "Maybe not to the untrained eye."

"Well," I said contentiously, "what's so interesting about it?"

He didn't reply to this directly. Instead he said, "You know, some of these wrecks date back one hell of a long time." He gazed down at the untasted beer. "In fact," he continued, looking up so that his faded blue eyes met mine, "there is one wreck off the coast in Kent that dates back to the Bronze Age, so they reckon."

"Really?" I said.

He nodded seriously. "Some of these wrecks . . . " His voice trailed off and his gaze drifted away from mine, as though seeking something. Then with an effort he continued, "Some of them date right back to the time when people used to worship the sea . . . "

"And you reckon this is one of them, do you?" I asked.

"Who can say?" he said in a very un-Daffy-like voice. He sounded dreamy, unfocussed. "Who can say . . . ?" he repeated. He hugged himself, seemingly cold again, and I saw a tear well up at the corner of his left eye. It spilled over and ran down his cheek. I could have sworn that it had a tinge of grey-green in it, that it was not clear, as tears should be. Then I looked away, embarrassed at this apparent display of emotion, and sat studying my fingernails for a minute or two.

"I'll go and get a drink," I said in the end. I didn't offer Daffy one; it was going to take him all night to drink that pint at this rate. I took my time up at the bar, wanting to give him time to pull himself together, and when I got back to the corner, he had gone. The pint of bitter was still standing, reproachfully untasted, on a pristine beermat.

I didn't see Daffy again for a couple of weeks after that, but I did run into Gormless Gavin. I'd been to the dive shop, hoping to pick up an American magazine they'd got on order for me. Rather to my surprise (it was the middle of Saturday morning) the shop was closed; *very* closed, I should say—there was not even a notice to say when it would be open again. I guessed anyone who had tried to come in for an air fill would be cursing Daffy.

After a bit of aimless strolling I stuck my head into Daffy's local, thinking I might catch him in there. No Daffy; but Gavin was propping the bar up, looking as dim-witted as usual, his baseball cap on back-to-front in a way that was probably meant to look raffish, but fell sadly short of the mark. I went up to him and said, "Hello, Gavin—remember me?" Then seeing the look with which this remark was greeted, I wondered whether he was stupid enough to think I was giving him the come-on, so I followed up swiftly with, "I'm looking for Daffy. Any idea where he is?"

Gavin shook his head and said what sounded like "Fuh"—as though he wanted to swear but couldn't be bothered to get the whole word out. "I don't work for him no more," he added balefully.

"Oh," I said, disconcerted. Whilst I was wondering how to follow up this remark the barman wafted over, and on impulse I offered Gavin a pint. He gave me that look again, but he wasn't going to refuse a free drink—especially not now that he was newly unemployed.

"Cheers," he said, consuming a fair proportion of it in the first gulp.

I waited until he had put the glass back on the bar, and then I said, "The fact is, er, Gavin—well, I'm concerned about Daffy. Is he still diving on his own?"

I had hoped for some information, perhaps even some reassurance that Daffy had been busy with some more conventional diving trips. Instead I got a splutter which would have covered me in regurgitated beer if I were a little less quick on my feet, and then a torrent of Gavin-speak, from which I eventually discerned that not only was Daffy still diving on his own, but he was diving *exclusively* on his own—all other trips having been abandoned—and always at the same dive site. Do you need me to tell you which one it was? It was that blasted wreck at twenty metres. Well, that was bad enough—Daffy had evidently succumbed to some sort of obsession—but what followed was worse.

Gavin claimed Daffy had been staying down for stretches of more than two and a half hours at a time. And he said the time was getting longer with each dive. The first time Daffy had been down for longer than an hour Gavin had fidgeted about on the boat, wondering whether to call the coastguard, and alternately dithering and panicking. He suspected it was some sort of a trick to wind him up;

Daffy had a second bottle hidden somewhere, or had surfaced out of sight somewhere when he was supposedly on the bottom. But one way or another, Gavin didn't like it; it had him spooked. "Fuh," he said several times, shaking his head at the remembrance. Finally he had argued with Daffy, and in the end of it was, they parted company. I didn't know what to make of any of this, but at least with his boat handler gone, I reckoned that would stop Daffy doing any more of these insane solo dives for a bit. Just goes to show how wrong you can be . . .

It must have been about the middle of July when I passed the actual wreck site where Daffy had allegedly been carrying out his impossibly-long dives. I'd visited it in my mind quite a few times, of course, wondering why Daffy felt drawn to it, and thinking about those posts sticking up out of the sand, totally bare of all sea life, not even a barnacle. But this was the first time I'd actually passed over it again. I was with the club this time, and as it happened we were going to dive the *Callisto*, the wreck Daffy and I had been going to do, the day we first dived that thing at twenty metres. I was standing in the cabin of the boat, looking ahead, so I was the first one to see it. The rib, I mean. A little blob of bright orange bobbing up and down on its own amongst the waves. When I say *on its own*, I speak advisedly. As far as I could tell, there was no-one in it. I spoke to the boat handler and we slowed down for a closer look.

Sure enough, there was the boat without a soul in it. I won't make the obvious *Mary Celeste* comparison because apart from anything else, this thing was not much bigger than a dinghy. But it gave me a cold feeling all the same, seeing it riding the waves there, with no-one on board. There was a stout line attached to the front of it, leading down into the water. It was taut, so I guess the rib had been anchored. At any rate it was not going anywhere, just drifting in a lazy arc with the current. I can't absolutely swear to it, of course, since I didn't have any sort of bearing, but I was certain it was anchored over that twenty metre dive site.

Well, we debated what to do, because this wasn't the normal sort of thing to come across. Some of the others came up with theories: there were divers down, and the boat handler had fallen overboard and drowned. Or there were divers down, and the damn-fools hadn't left anyone on the rib in the first place. But nobody suggested what I suspected, which was that there was one diver down, and there had never been anybody else involved at all. In the end we radioed the coastguard who said they'd check it out, though what they proposed to do I can't imagine. Then we went on our way. When we passed back over the site later on the rib had gone, so there was general relief and a lot of superior comments about poor diving practice.

It was another ten days before I saw that rib again. This time it was at a temporary mooring on the quayside leading into the marina, and in the bottom was an untidy jumble of diving gear. Standing on the quay, bending over a bottle which he was unstrapping from his stab jacket, was Daffy. He was still in his semi-dry suit. I stared at the rib, and then at Daffy, and my heart sank. Maybe he heard me exhale or something, but he looked up and for a moment he just gazed at me, as though he didn't recognise me at all. He looked grey again; I noticed his lips looked almost blue. But then suddenly his face broke into that familiar grin and he said, "About time too," as though he had been expecting me, and then: "You can give me a hand with this lot." He hopped back into the rib and started passing things out to me: a weight belt with great hunks of metal threaded onto a kevlar strap, so that it looked like some sort of gigantic charm bracelet; a mask with a snorkel fitted into the strap; his octopus rig, looking like its namesake, shiny black tubing legs sprouting everywhere. His dive computer, carefully wrapped in a netting goody bag.

Whilst Daffy was fiddling around with the dry box under the rib's one seat, looking no doubt for his keyring, I slid the computer out of the net bag. I was curious, I admit it; I didn't think for one moment that Daffy had *really* been underwater for two-and-a-half hours—we used to joke that Daffy had gills, but even *he* couldn't do the impossible—but I did wonder just how long he *had* been down, and whether he had been taking risks with his decompression times. Daffy had a similar model of computer to my own. At the moment it was just displaying a surface time, but a couple of button-presses later I had his last dive time, and the times of the three dives before that. To say I was astounded would be the biggest understatement since Noah looked up and said it looked like rain. According to the computer, Daffy's last dive had lasted not two-and-a-half, but *six* hours. The one before that had apparently lasted five hours and forty minutes, and the other two were between four and five hours. All totally impossible. The depth was the same for all of them: twenty metres. Well, *no-one* stays twenty metres underwater for *that* long. Even if you had an unending supply of air, the dive would be right outside any known sport-diving decompression tables, and the decompression stops would be ludicrous. The dive computer didn't like it any more than I did: several very ominous-looking symbols were flashing away on the little screen. I looked down at the readout and then at Daffy. I couldn't believe he was standing there in front of me.

At that moment he looked up, and his face instantly darkened.

"What are you fooling around with that for?" He was on the quayside in an instant and had ripped the computer out of my hands. I simply gaped at him.

"It's on the blink," he snapped. "Don't make it any bloody worse by fiddling around with it."

"But Daffy . . . " I stuttered.

"No buts," he began, and then he stopped. A sort of tremor seemed to pass through him, and a strangely unfocussed look came into his eyes. Then suddenly water, greyish-green water, was gushing from his nose, pouring out of each nostril. He made a choking, gargling sound, and put a hand up to his face. Water ran between his fingers and down the back of his hand. It looked tainted, viscous.

"Shit, Daffy . . . " I dithered, not knowing what to do to help him. But before I could do anything at all, the attack—or whatever it was—had passed. Daffy was wiping his nose with one neoprene-clad forearm. He shook his head, as though trying to get water out of his ears. Then, incredibly, he gave me a broad grin.

"Better out than in," he said, and actually laughed.

Well, I didn't stick around after that. The whole thing had freaked me out far too much. Somewhat later in the evening it occurred to me that there *might* be some logical explanation for what I had seen on the dive computer; supposing, for example, Daffy had lost the computer on a first dive, and then by some incredible piece of luck had picked it up again at the same dive site hours later? Still, I had to concede, it was stretching the imagination somewhat to think that he might have done that *four* times. Perhaps the computer *was* on the blink. No-one stays at twenty metres for *six hours*.

I did see Daffy again, but not until August; late in August, starting to approach the end of the diving season. I'd been to the shop on numerous occasions, but it was always closed. Inevitably custom went elsewhere, to the fancy new place two miles up the coast. The shop started to develop a dilapidated look; someone had cracked a pane of glass in the door, and it stayed cracked. A sheaf of free newspapers, which had been crammed into the letterbox, became soaked with rain and turned into a drooping pulp. Dead insects appeared amongst the items displayed in the windows.

Daffy's boat seemed to be permanently at its mooring in the marina. There was a shabby blue tarpaulin cover over it, with a puddle of rainwater on top. It, too, looked as though it had not been visited by its owner for months. Still, Daffy was taking the rib out—other members of the club I belonged to mentioned seeing him in it, either speeding out towards that twenty metre dive site, or loading and unloading equipment at the quayside. No-one seemed to have spoken to him—or perhaps they did not care to repeat the conversations, knowing that I was a friend of his. Once it had got around that the rib we had seen apparently abandoned at sea was Daffy's, there was inevitably comment about it, but it swiftly dried up whenever I appeared. So for a while all I heard about Daffy was second-hand, and when that source of information dried up, he might just as well have disappeared into the sea, the green water have closed over his head leaving no trace.

At last, one evening, I was walking back to my flat, taking a route which allowed a pleasant view of the quayside, the water sparkling with the last dying rays of the sun, when I saw someone close to the water; the figure seemed in fact to be *in the water*, until I realised that he or she was standing in some small craft below the level of the quayside, and was unloading something onto the stones. *Daffy*, I thought, and on impulse I cut across the intervening ground and onto the quayside.

"Daffy! *Daffy!*" I called in a cheerful voice as I drew nearer. He looked up, and the words died in my throat. As God is my witness, I have never seen another human being look as bad as Daffy did at that moment. Everything about him seemed grey: his skin, his hair, even the faded semi-dry suit he was wearing, which had an odd mildewed look about it, as though some strange lichenous growth had taken root in it. His flesh, which had the same lifeless colour about it, looked soft and puffy in an oddly repulsive way, like some sort of pallid fungus which has grown in a dark damp place. Out of eye sockets, which were deeply ringed in purple the colour of bruises, Daffy's eyes gazed through me unseeingly. Even the cornflower colour of the irises seemed to have succumbed to the same greying effect; no longer blue, they appeared grey-green, dull like pieces of glass which have been tumbled by the ocean until they are perfectly smooth and opaque. He stretched out a hand towards me, groping blindly; it was like a sea sponge, the white fingers waterlogged and flabby. Involuntarily I took a step backwards.

"Daffy—my God, what happened to you?" I choked out.

No expression passed over that grey and flabby face; the lips did not move, the mouth did not open. But I swear to you that I heard his voice all the same, heard it in my mind as clearly as if he had spoken. He said: *She still sails the seas.*

Then with appalling slackness his jaw dropped open, and water *poured* out, it gushed out in a grey-green torrent, mixed with a thickish yellow scum and stinking of brine. The lichenous semi-dry suit shone with wet; the dead-white fingers groping uselessly in the air were slick with it; water streamed off Daffy's body and pooled on the worn stones of the quay. When at last the vomitus ceased I looked at him, aghast, and saw that in his salt-encrusted hair tiny creatures were crawling. One fell, sliding unheeded down the planes of his face and dropping onto the stones, where I saw with revulsion that it was a tiny albino crab. With an exclamation of disgust, I crushed it with my shoe. I looked back at Daffy, at those dull inhuman eyes which seemed to see, not me, but something far, far away.

"I—I'll get help," I said, and then I fled. I turned once and he was still standing there on the quay, a dark shape in the fading light, faintly shining with the wet. Then I half-ran back to my flat without looking back again.

I never saw Daffy again. It was Gavin who found him—Gormless Gavin—who to all appearances was utterly lacking in energy and initiative, but who nevertheless broke into Daffy's shop late one afternoon in September, allegedly looking for a last pay packet Daffy had never given him. Stepping over the piles of junk mail, red bills and free newspapers, not to mention a few mouse droppings, Gavin had paused in his mercenary mission, scenting something odd on the air, something a lot fouler than mouse excreta. It had smelt odd enough for him to go up the back stairs to Daffy's flat above the shop, where the front door stood wide open and the smell grew thick and poisonously sweet. He had called Daffy's name, and receiving no reply, he had gone inside . . .

Daffy lay on the floor, still dressed in his semi-dry suit; in fact the tight layer of neoprene had done much to preserve the body. The post-mortem determined that he had been dead for some three to four months. The body was not a pretty sight, of course, after so much time, but what was worst was that much of the exposed flesh seemed to have been eaten away, much as you might have expected to see if the body had been abandoned to the mercy of fish and other sea creatures; ragged holes in the pulpy flesh were all that remained of Daffy's cornflower blue eyes. In so far as it was possible to ascertain the cause of death with the body in a state of decomposition, it was thought that Daffy had died of drowning; the condition of the body was consistent with its having been in the water for a long period. But as to how it came to be inside Daffy's flat, and what motivation any third party could have for removing a dead body to such a place, there was a blank. There was no detectable evidence of foul play.

I sometimes go down to the beach on my own these days and sit on the shingle looking out to sea, out towards the unmarked and uncharted spot where Daffy and I first discovered that wreck, or whatever it might be, at twenty metres' depth. I don't suppose I shall ever know now what manner of thing it was, or how old it was, and I'm glad of that. It's quite true, you know: there are a few wrecks found which date back to mediaeval times, or Roman times, or even earlier. To the Bronze Age, when maybe people did worship the sea.

I think about my friend, Daffy. I think about his smile, and his blue eyes, faded by the sea and the sun, and about the mad ideas he used to have. But mostly I think about his last words to me. *She still sails the seas.* What did he mean? For *she* did he mean the wreck itself? Or did he mean some *other* thing, some personality real or imagined—some siren of the deep?

And each windy day I look to the heavens and watch for the black clouds scudding across the sky, for the clouds that herald the storm which will lash the land and make the sea boil again; the storm whose power will reach down even to the bed of the sea, and bury that thing again.

The Game of Bear

Two elderly persons sat reading and smoking in the library of a country house after tea on an afternoon in the Christmas holidays, and outside a number of the children of the house were playing about. They had turned out all the lights and were engaged in the dreadful game of "Bear" which entails stealthy creepings up and down staircases and along passages, and being leapt upon from doorways with loud and hideous cries. Such a cry, and an answering scream of great poignancy, were heard just outside the library door. One of the two readers—an uncle of the young things who were disporting themselves there—leapt from his chair and dashed the door open. "I will *not* have you doing that!" he shouted (and his voice was vibrant with real anger); "do you hear? Stop it at once. I can't stand it. You—you—Why can't you find something else? What? . . . Well, I don't care, I can't put up with it . . . Yes, very well, go and do it somewhere where I can't hear it." He subsided into a growl and came back to his chair; but his friend saw that his nerves were really on edge, and ventured something sympathetic. "It's all very well," said the uncle, "but I can *not* bear that jumping out and screaming. Stupid of me to fly out like that, but I couldn't help it. It reminded me of all that business—*you* know."

"Well," said the friend after a short pause, "I'm really not sure that I do. Oh!" he added, in a more concerned tone, "unless you mean Purdue." "That's it," said the uncle. There was another silence, and then the friend said, "Really, I'm not sorry that happened just now, for I never did hear the rights of the Purdue business. Will you tell me exactly what happened?"

"I don't know," said the uncle: "I *really* don't know, if I ought. But I think I will. Not just now, though. I'll tell you what: if it's fine tomorrow we'll take a walk in the morning; and tonight I'll think over the whole affair and get it straight in my mind. I *have* often felt somebody besides me ought to know about it, and all his people are out of the way now."

The next day *was* fine, and the two men walked out to a hill at no real distance, which was known as Windmill Hill. The mill that had topped it was gone but a bit of the brick foundation remained and afforded a seat from which a good stretch of pleasant wild country could be seen. Here then Mr. A and Mr. B sat down on the short, dry grass with their backs against the warm brick wall, and Mr. A produced a little bundle of folded paper and a pocketbook which he held up before Mr. B as an indication that he was prepared not only to tell the story to which he stood pledged, but to back it with documentary evidence.

"I brought you here," he said, "partly because you can see Purdue's place. There!" He pointed with his stick to a wooded slope which might be three or four miles off. In the wood was a large clearing and in the clearing stood a mansion of yellow stone with a portico, upon which, as it chanced, the sun was shining very brilliantly, so that the house stood out brightly against the background of dark trees.

"Where shall I begin?" said Mr. A.

"Why," said Mr. B, "I'll tell you exactly how little I know, and then you can judge. You and Purdue, you remember, were senior to me at school and at Cambridge. He went down after his three years; you stayed up for part of a fourth, and then I began to see more of you: before that, I was more with people of my own year, and, beyond a fair number of meetings with Purdue at breakfast and lunch and so on, I never saw much of him—not nearly as much as I should have liked, in fact. Then I remember your going to stay with him—there, I suppose" (pointing with his stick)—"in the Easter Vac, and—well, that was the last of it."

"Just so," said Mr. A; "I didn't come up again, and you and I practically didn't meet till a year or two back, did we? Though you were a better correspondent than any of my other Cambridge friends. Very well, then, there it is: I was never inclined to write the story down in a letter, and the long and short of it is that you have never heard it: but you do know what sort of man Purdue was, and how fond I was of him.

"When I stayed with him over there, the place was his only home, and yet it wasn't his. He was an orphan and practically adopted by his uncle and aunt who were quite old childless people. There had been another uncle who had married a village woman, and had one daughter. That couple were very odd squalid creatures, and died off, I think from drink, but the daughter survived and went on living in a cottage in the next parish. She wasn't left destitute by any means in the way of money; but she lived all by herself, and I think always with a sense of injury upon her that she wasn't noticed by the county families and such. The remaining uncle and aunt had been kind enough to her and at one time used to invite her over to their place, but she had a very difficult temper and was always on the look-out for slights and injuries, and at last they gave up the effort to be cordial, and saw no more of her. It wasn't to be expected after that that they would pass on the property to her (it was entirely at their disposition, to do what they liked with it) and no more they did. When they died it went to Purdue, about a year before his own death, that was.

"So there he was, settled, you would say, into a happy life: he'd been brought up in the country and knew all the neighbourhood, places and people, very well; and was interested in farming and forestry and prepared to make himself useful. The visit I paid him that Christmas was particularly delightful: he was on such excellent terms with everybody in the village. 'Master Henry' to all of them, and just as well liked by the neighbours in the larger houses. I think the only fly in the ointment was that woman Caroline Purdue. She had taken to attending our parish church and we used to find her in our pew every Sunday morning. She didn't say much to Henry, but all the service time she sat and looked at him through her veil. A short stout red-faced woman she was, with black hair and snappy black eyes. She used to wait in the churchyard till we had gone out and then set off on her three mile walk home. She gave me the creeps, I couldn't say why; I suppose there was a flavour of concentrated hostility about her.

"Henry was anxious of something of the same kind. His lawyer told me after his death that he had tried through them to get her to accept a handsome addition to her income and the gift of a suitable house wherever she liked in some other part of the county. They said she was as impracticable a woman as they had ever come across: she just sat and smiled broadly at them and said she was quite comfortable where she was, and didn't want to move out of reach of her cousin Henry. 'But wouldn't it be more lively and amusing for you to be in some place where there's more to be seen—theatres, and that sort of thing?' No, oh no, she had plenty of things to occupy herself with: and—again—she didn't want to move out of reach of her cousin Henry.

" 'But, but: your cousin Henry, you know; he's likely to be a busy man—travelling about a good deal, and occupied with his men friends: it isn't probable that he'll be able to see much of you.' Oh, she was quite content to take her chance of that: they would often be meeting when he was riding about, and no doubt there would be times when he was alone at the Court, and she could look in on him. 'Ah well, that's just the point. Are you sure that Mr. Purdue will welcome that?' 'Yes, to be sure, why not?' 'Well, we have reason to think that he doesn't wish it.' Oh indeed! and pray had he commissioned these gentlemen to tell his own cousin that he had cast her off? A nice thing for a relative to hear, that her own flesh and blood preferred not to have anything to do with her. What had she done, she should like to know, to be treated in that way?

"There was more to the same effect, and the storm rose quickly, culminating in a short burst of tears, and a rapid stumping out of the room. The gentlemen who had been conducting the interview were left looking at each other and feeling they had not done much to advance their client's wishes. But at least Miss Purdue left off her attendance at our church, and, we gathered, did not favour any other place of worship in its stead.

"She was not more popular with the rest of the community than with Henry.

"How is the rest of this to be told? I have here some papers which bear on it, but they are fragmentary, of course. When Henry Purdue was alone in that big house he did what at other times was rather foreign to his habits— confided his feelings to paper. Here are some entries."

" 'Letter from C.P.' (Caroline Purdue, of course). 'Infernal woman. May she come and see me and talk over this painful matter. No, she mayn't.'

"This was dated January 18—.

"Another entry from the same month reads, 'Lunch with Ferrars (Henry's lawyer) was disturbed by the arrival of C.P., who presented herself at the front door and was with difficulty persuaded to leave. Cannot think how she got past the gate; she is known to everyone on the estate.'

"February 20, 18—: 'Another letter from C.P. Burnt it without opening.'

"There are more entries like these," said Mr. A. "I shan't read them all. Miss Purdue seems to have been an unusually persistent person; rebuffs only made her the more determined. When her attempts to gain access to Henry failed, she clearly decided to try another tack."

He drew out another paper. "Look here. March 3rd, 18—: 'Dixon came up from the gatehouse at lunchtime with a brace of pheasants, saying that Miss Purdue had sent them. Wretched creature! Of course it was too late to send them back, and I was hard put to know what to do with them; I had no intention of eating them myself. In the end I told him to throw them out.'

"That was shortly before the end of term. Henry had written to me asking me to go to him for the Easter Vac. I had thought of visiting some of my own people, but Henry's invitation was urgent; he said he had some matter over which he particularly wished to ask my advice. There was an anxious, insistent tone to his letter which was quite unlike Henry. Of course I said I would go.

"When I got there I found Henry rather thinner than when I had last seen him, but very much the same Henry as ever, except that he seemed a little irritable. There was an incident on the day I arrived—I couldn't make much of it at the time. We went into the drawing-room for tea and there was a large vase on one of the tables, full of those white flowers—what do they call them?—Easter lilies. Henry seemed struck by them and asked the girl who was setting out the tea things where they had come from. She was sure she couldn't say; she thought someone had delivered them. There was no note.

"Henry seemed unaccountably annoyed by this reply. He paced twice up and down the room with a thunderous face, and then he seized the lilies out of the vase, and strode over to the window, where he hurled the lot out into the shrubbery. The girl was open-mouthed and I uttered a word or two of remonstrance, which Henry did not appear to hear. He said something under his breath, something like—*she shan't*—and then he flung himself down into a chair and put a hand to his brow.

" 'I suppose you think I have taken leave of my senses,' he said when the girl had left the room. He gave a short laugh. 'The truth is, I'm not too sure that I haven't. It's that—woman. The one who styles herself my cousin. Well,' he added with sudden energy, 'Cousin Henry is not at home to visitors—not now—not ever. She can send what she likes.'

"I ventured to ask whether the lilies had come from Miss Purdue.

" 'Of course they did,' said Henry impatiently. 'But she needn't think she can frighten me like that.'

"The offending flowers had certainly had a somewhat funereal appearance, but it was hard to see how they could be perceived as a form of intimidation. I tried to hint as much but Henry was unusually touchy and inclined to snap at me. The lilies were not the first present which Miss Purdue had sent to the Court, he said; she was always sending things. At first he had thought she was trying to ingratiate herself, but now—now she was becoming a nuisance, and he wouldn't have it!

"There was a fretful tone in his voice which was quite new to me. Henry had always been a level-headed sort of person, not the type to allow himself to be upset by such a thing. I remembered the letter he had sent me, and wondered whether the matter of Miss Purdue was the thing about which he had wished to consult me. When I asked him directly about it, he was at first very reluctant to get to the point, but eventually he told me a very curious story.

"It seems that Miss Purdue had indeed been sending things to the Court—all sorts of items—with the compliments of his cousin; once it was a brace of pheasants, another time a bottle of some evil-looking beverage which Henry had immediately thrown out. After a while the accompanying messages had stopped, but items had continued to arrive, which Henry assumed had originated with Miss Purdue. He felt convinced, he said, that she had given up trying to make friends with him, and that now she had quite another motive; he thought she was trying to introduce something into the house.

" 'I know how ridiculous that sounds,' he said, 'But I can't shake the idea. Why, just yesterday there was a ragged little girl came to the back door and offered the cook a bunch of herbs, but she wouldn't take anything for them.'

" 'I should like to have such hawkers coming to me,' I said, trying to lift his mood, but Henry didn't smile.

" 'No, you wouldn't,' he said. He gave a long sigh. 'That's not the end of it, A—. A couple of weeks ago the rector—Dr. Bertram, you remember him—was invited to dine with me. Well, at the last minute he sent to say that he would be unavoidably delayed, and when he did eventually arrive he was obviously upset. We sat down to dinner and he hummed and haw'd for a while before he came to the point. He said that someone had been in the churchyard and had disturbed one of the graves—dug about in it, he said. The soil was all heaped up as though the grave had just been freshly turned. He couldn't say whether anything had been damaged or removed; he hardly cared to disturb it any further. He had simply told old Bowes—the sexton—to make it neat again.

" 'Dr. Bertram's embarrassment was so obvious that even before he told me, I had guessed whose grave it was which had been desecrated; it was that of my uncle Purdue. Shocked as I was, my mind sprang immediately to Caroline Purdue.'

"Henry paused.

" 'Surely you don't suggest that your cousin had anything to do with it?' I said.

" 'I do,' he said. 'My uncle hadn't an enemy in the world. Besides, I was not the only one who jumped to that conclusion. She is not well-liked in the village, you know. Dr. Bertram told me that old Bowes had said it must be her; always hanging about, he said, though she never attended the services any more like a Christian person. Dr. Bertram had been unable to stop him blabbering about it, and eventually someone had gone to Miss Purdue's cottage, but found it all shut up; it looked as though she had gone away, he said.

" 'In the absence of any definite proof it hardly seemed right to summon the constable, so Dr. Bertram and I determined to ride out there ourselves the next morning and speak to Miss Purdue. At any rate it seemed she had got her wish at last, for she could expect a visit from her Cousin Henry—though I doubted she would like what her affectionate cousin had to say. When we got there, however, we found that the cottage was indeed shut up, and it looked as though it had been so for some time. We asked about, and nobody had seen her in recent days, but none of her neighbours could say where she had gone; she kept herself to herself, they said.'

" 'At any rate, you are well rid of her,' I said.

" 'That's just it. I don't think I *am* rid of her,' said Henry. 'I can't shake the feeling that she's trying to get at me, somehow. The things she keeps sending—'

" 'The things,' I interrupted, 'which may or may not be from her. Your cousin may very well be established at Bournemouth, in which case the next gift you can expect will be some horrid souvenir.'

"Henry didn't laugh.

" 'If she succeeds—' he said, 'What then?'

" 'Then nothing,' I retorted robustly. 'Put it out of your mind.'

"I'm not sure that Henry did succeed in putting the matter out of his mind, but at any rate he had composed himself, and the rest of the day passed off without incident.

"It must have been about a week later that I noticed a change in Henry's manner, a gradual dropping-off in spirits. He seemed unaccountably nervous, and his tendency to irritability erupted several times into actual anger over some trivial thing—a dish which was not to his taste, an unmarked parcel which turned out to be nothing more alarming than a couple of old books sent over on approval. On one occasion he worked himself up into a rage over—of all things—the kitchen cat, which he said should be drowned if it didn't keep the rats down. The housekeeper ventured to say that, begging Mr. Purdue's pardon, so far as she knew, there *were* no rats in the Court. 'Of course there are,' retorted Henry. 'I hear them in the passage at night—pattering up and down.'

"In Henry's overwrought state of mind there seemed a definite risk that he might really try to drown the wretched cat himself. I interposed with a suggestion that he have the gamekeeper's terrier brought into the house to look for the offending vermin. As soon as we were alone I spoke to him quite plainly, and asked him what was troubling him.

"He seemed positively relieved to be asked. He wouldn't have told anyone else, he said, not even Dr. Bertram— they would think he was mad. He said he had a peculiar feeling all the time of being watched; he thought it had started about a week before, though he couldn't say why— nothing in particular had occurred at that time.

" 'No—not *watched*,' he said. '*Stalked*. I feel somehow that I am never quite alone. It's worse at night, you know. The passage is so damnably dark. I feel as though I were playing that abominable game that children play—yes, that's it—*Bear*. At the turn of the staircase I always have a very distinct feeling that something is waiting in the darkness at the top—waiting to spring upon me.' He gave a sigh which was terrible to hear.

"Of course I did my best to talk him out of what seemed a morbidly imaginative state of mind. 'A good night's sleep will cure you of fancies of that sort,' I told him roundly.

"Henry gave a bitter laugh. 'A good night's sleep? Yes— if I could only stop myself from dreaming.'

"I thought little of this at the time, but a couple of evenings later, when we were in the library together, digesting a rather indifferent dinner with the assistance of some very good cigars, Henry brought up the subject again. I had noticed that as the hour grew later, Henry had become restless; he glanced at the clock on the mantelpiece every few minutes, and lingered interminably over his brandy. Clearly something was on his mind, and eventually he resolved to speak.

"He introduced the subject in a roundabout way, by asking me whether I had read Macrobius's *Commentarii in Somnium Scipionis*, and what I thought of it.

"As you know, that was not really my field, but as it happens I had read parts of it. I said I supposed it was interesting, in its way.

" 'Interesting?' said Henry, looking at me somewhat sharply. 'Yes, certainly it is interesting—but you don't think there is anything in it?'

" 'Certainly there is something in it,' I said. 'Doesn't he say that most dreams are caused by overindulging in food and drink?'

" '*Some* dreams,' Henry corrected me rather irritably. 'Others he says are oracular or actually prophetic.'

" 'And some are simply nightmares,' I pointed out.

" 'Yes,' said Henry eagerly. 'But how to tell which is which?—that is the question.' He shook his head.

"I had nothing to say to this; it was clearly not the moment to tell Henry that I thought the idea of prophetic dreams preposterous, so I smoked for a while in silence and waited for him to go on, which he eventually did. It will not come as a surprise to you that Henry himself was suffering from unpleasant dreams—or rather, I should say, from one dream, which recurred with painful regularity. Henry said that in the dream he always found himself outside the closed door of his own bedroom, but that either he found himself in the person of someone else or he was somehow outside his own body, for he always had the conviction that he—Henry—was asleep in bed on the other side of the door. The passage was very dark so that one could hardly have made out anyone who came down it, but all the same (Henry said) he thought he could perceive movement at the other end of it. He did not think it was a person—quite—although it was about the size of one; it was too dreadfully thin and from the way it moved he surmised that there was something odd about its limbs—either there were too many joints or some of them bent the wrong way—he could not really say. It seemed to come on with a lurching, scuttling gait like a gigantic spider, with the ends of the limbs scrabbling energetically at the walls.

"Henry said that the sight of this creature was nearly enough to send him out of his wits, and yet it never attempted any sort of attack upon him—somehow he knew that its intentions were focussed upon the person lying in the bed behind the closed door. He would always wake up before the thing reached the door—or else the dream would pass away into some other nonsensical scene. The whole dream was disgusting enough, Henry said, but the worst of it was, the thing he saw was *hungry*.

"When he finished speaking, he looked at me expectantly, and I was forced to say something or other about dreams going by contraries, which sounded lame enough.

" 'No, no,' he said. 'It is not to be explained away as easily as *that*. I am convinced there is malice in it. But how—,' he went on, more to himself than to me, '—how she got it in, I cannot think.'

"*She* I took to be his troublesome cousin, Caroline Purdue. There was no possible reply to this; I could not conceive that his cousin was responsible for the dreams, except in as much as the thought of her weighed upon Henry's mind. Soon after that we parted for the night.

"About an hour and a half later, I was torn abruptly from a deep sleep by the sound of a door slamming close by. The next second there came a scream—I can't begin to describe it to you. It sounded as though someone were undergoing the most hideous tortures—a mixture of mortal pain and terrible fear.

"For several seconds I lay paralysed in the bed, too stricken with horror to move. Then as the scream died away I pulled myself together and leapt up. I snatched up a heavy candlestick to use as a weapon if need be, and ran out into the passage. A moment later I felt myself thrust aside as easily as if I had been a child, by someone who moved with the rough energy of a beast. Staggering back against the panelling, I saw a shaft of moonlight coming through the narrow window fall onto the head and the shoulders. I could not help uttering a cry of disgust. The next instant the figure had been swallowed again by the dark.

"Stumbling towards Henry's door, I saw his housekeeper at the top of the stairs. She had thrown a shawl around her shoulders and carried a lamp, which threw a yellowish light onto features rendered almost stupid by terror.

" 'Here—give me that lamp,' I snapped at her. '*Henry*—?' I called in a louder tone. There was no reply, although his door stood half-open. I suppose I knew what I should find before I entered the room.

"I don't know what Henry had been doing when that thing found him. A number of books were strewn about the floor, amidst the smashed remains of a lamp. It was a miracle the place had not been set alight. Henry himself—what remained of him—was on the bed, the sheets of which were pulled and dragged about as though a desperate struggle had taken place. The bed-curtains on one side of it had been half ripped down. I took one look at that brown and shrunken face and turned aside with a stifled oath.

"The housekeeper had no such restraint. 'Master's been turned into a monkey!' she screamed, and instantly went into hysterics. By this time Henry's man had arrived, and between us we got her and the other servants out of the room and closed the door. There was nothing we could do for Henry, of course.

"You will ask me what it was that pushed past me in the passage. I can only tell you this. Henry said the thing which frightened him so much in his dreams was *thin*, but this was *fat*. The head—I only saw it from the back, not the face, for which I am profoundly grateful—and the shoulders were bare, and so swollen that the flesh had a greasy shine to it. So grotesquely bloated was it that no neck was discernible, only a deep crease between head and trunk. Henry had said he thought the thing was hungry. Now it was no longer hungry; it was *full*.

"Of course there was an enquiry. I contributed what I could. Henry's falling-out—if you can call it that—with Caroline Purdue was well-known locally, but the woman herself could not be traced, nor was she to be found at any time afterwards. I confirmed that Henry had anticipated some nuisance from his easily-offended cousin, but that I had not recognised Henry's assailant. I could not give a full description of course; I said I thought the person was corpulent.

"The day after Henry's death I went to Henry's room again, to perform what last little service I could for my poor friend, by picking up and ordering the books which had been strewn about the floor. I found the housekeeper in the room; I think she had come to put down the blinds. As I entered I heard her make a little exclamation.

" 'Begging your pardon, Mr. A—,' she said. 'I really can't think what *this* is doing here.' She indicated an inoffensive-looking plant in a rather ornate pot. It might have been an oriental ginger jar—it had rather that look. It was sitting on the window-ledge, mostly hidden by the curtain.

" 'Not a very pretty thing,' I agreed.

" 'It's basil, sir,' she said in an indignant tone. I suppose the events of the previous night had told on her nerves, because she was not content until she had summoned several of the housemaids and asked them who had put a pot of basil in the master's bedroom; *she* had certainly not placed it there. Eventually it was established that the newest girl had put it there a day or two before, thinking it was some sort of house plant. The housekeeper rolled her eyes significantly at this evidence of ignorance. Where had she got it from? she insisted upon knowing. After some hesitation, the girl explained that someone had brought the plant to the back door—no, she couldn't say who—not even if it had been a man or a woman. She didn't think much of it at the time. It seemed that she had only been employed at the house for a few days and was not aware of Henry's instructions regarding the acceptance of unexpected deliveries. She had thought the pot pretty, and had taken the liberty of setting it there in the window. She hadn't thought that she was doing anything wrong—! It was apparent that the girl was close to tears. The housekeeper relented.

" 'Well, well,' she said, 'It can't bother the master now. But you can take it down to the kitchen. Look lively now.'

"The girl made to pick up the pot, but whether she was clumsy or simply nervous, it slipped out of her hands and smashed to pieces on the floor. I hardly took in the housekeeper's fresh cries of vexation. Something lay there amongst the shards of broken pottery and clumps of earth—something I did not like to touch with my bare hands. In the end I got out my handkerchief and picked it up using that. It was a little bundle of bones and what looked like twigs, tied together with a ragged and discoloured piece of ribbon. The twigs were much scratched about, as though someone had tried to carve

59

a pattern into them, but it was inexpertly done. I could make no sense of it.

"Later that day I rode over to Dr. Bertram's and showed him the little bundle. He looked at them for a long time, and then he looked at me.

" 'We had better tell the servants they were *animal* bones,' he said. 'And I shall ask Bowes—no, bother the man, he won't be able to keep his mouth shut. I shall deal with it myself. Well, well, A——, this is a very bad business. Poor Purdue.'

"Poor Henry indeed. After I left the Court, I suffered a nervous reaction to what had occurred. I never went back up to Cambridge; a change of scene recommended itself, and I went abroad, pleading my health. I recovered my spirits of course, though it was a long time before I felt quite comfortable in a strange house after dark, especially if there was no gas light.

"Still," said Mr. A, sliding the folded papers back into his pocket, "I can't forget that scream, you know—Henry's scream. However long I live I don't suppose I shall ever enjoy hearing anyone play that infernal game any more— the game of Bear."

Self Catering

Of course it's no use Watson complaining. It was all his fault in the first place; he was the one who told me I needed a holiday. I can remember it quite clearly—it was a grey wet Friday afternoon in March, and I was sitting in that cubbyhole of an office of mine going through a stack of invoices and sipping Margot's foul instant coffee out of a mug with a chip in it. Watson gave one of those irritatingly jaunty little double knocks on the door and came waltzing in without waiting for me to reply. As usual he was dressed a bit too flashily for Lorder & Son: he wore a double-breasted suit with a red silk handkerchief sticking out of the front pocket, and he had that jovial self-satisfied look on his well-fed face. "What're you up to then, Larkin?" he said without any introduction, and then he followed it up (as I knew he would) with that infuriating quip: "Still Larkin around?"

I did my best to ignore him but it didn't work. It never did: Watson had the hide of a rhinoceros. He came and perched on the corner of my desk and made a show of craning over to see what top-secret thing I was working on. When I didn't respond, he played his trump card. He said, "You're looking a bit peaky, Larkin. You want to watch it, old son, or one day you'll turn your toes up at that desk of yours. You should get out more." Well, he'd got me on my weak spot there. In those days I used to suffer a lot with my asthma, and immediately I started wondering if I'd been overdoing it. Was I really looking that bad? Watson saw my expression and pressed home his advantage. "You should take a holiday," he said impressively, flourishing a plump finger with an enormous signet ring at me.

"You don't need to tell me that," I said stiffly, and then I followed it up (I don't know why) with: "I'm going to book one this weekend, as a matter of fact."

Watson laughed that infuriating laugh of his. "That so?" he said. "I'll have to come round on Monday then and you can tell me all about it."

"I doubt you'd be interested," I replied as coldly as I could. "Our tastes are not the same."

"Ho ho," he laughed in that revoltingly hearty way. "Well, I'll see you on Monday then." He got off my desk with all the elegance of a water buffalo. "Keep Larkin around," was his parting shot before he took himself and his red silk handkerchief off somewhere else.

The trouble with people like Watson is that they do that, they force you into a corner. They goad you and goad you until you make some silly remark, and then you've committed yourself and you can't go back on it without making yourself look stupid. Of course I hadn't thought of taking a holiday before then, but now I had to book one before Monday. And then I couldn't help worrying a bit about what Watson had said. Did I *really* look peaky? Perhaps I *did* need a holiday. At any rate, the next morning saw me up bright and early, walking down the High Street looking for a travel agent. I'd never particularly looked for one before—I don't usually go on an organised holiday, I just spend a couple of weeks with my sister in Bournemouth. So this was a bit of a voyage of discovery, as you might say. The first one I went in to was no good at all. It was one of those chains, and it was all Ibiza this and Tenerife that—not at all suitable for a person of mature years and sober habits. I asked the girl on the desk if they did Swan Hellenic, and she stopped chewing her gum just long enough to say, "Where's that, then?"

After that I found myself out in the street again with no further ideas. I wandered about a bit, but didn't see anywhere else I could try, and frankly I was starting to worry about what Watson had said again. Perhaps all this walking around was stressing my body too. I decided that the best course of action would be to find a café and have a cup of tea and a bun whilst I plotted my next move. And that was how I found the place: I passed a side street with a little sign at the end of it reading "Jane's Coffee Shop"; I went down the street but I never got as far as Jane's because the first thing I came to was a travel agent.

I could see at once that this was a whole different kettle of fish from the last place. For starters, it didn't have that nasty flashy look that the other agent's had; there were no fluorescent yellow posters with "special offer" plastered all over them in the window; it looked neat and quiet and, well—staid. It looked like the place for gentleman travellers, not teenaged tourists. And secondly, the name painted over the quaint wooden door was a genuinely exotic one: "Cornelius Von Teufel, Travel Specialist", it read. You couldn't get more foreign than that. He was sure to be an expert on all things Continental. I pushed open the wooden door and went inside.

The door opening struck a little bell which jangled as I went into the shop—it was a nice old-fashioned touch, I thought. Almost as soon as the bell rang, a man wafted out from the back of the shop somewhere. His tread was so noiseless he might have been on castors. He was about sixty, I should say, and dressed in an immaculate dark grey suit, with a white shirt and a very sober dark tie. The only adornment was a little gold tie pin with some sort of funny little symbol on it. It created a very refined effect, as did his neat little beard, trimmed to a point. His hair was receding, revealing a high-domed forehead, but he had resisted the temptation to comb it over the bald patch. His eyes twinkled behind little steel-rimmed glasses.

"Cornelius Von Teufel," he said, in a soft and very slightly accented voice. He held out a perfectly manicured hand. "How may I help you?"

"Edward Larkin, pleased to meet you," I said, shaking his hand. "I'd like to book a holiday."

He made me a little bow. Really, his manners were perfectly gentlemanly, and I congratulated myself on finding the shop. It was a cut above the other place, that was for certain.

"You are, of course, aware that we specialise?" Von Teufel enquired.

"Well," I replied as grandly as I could, "I *am* looking for something, shall we say—exclusive." Then I added: "What sort of thing do you specialise in?"

"Spiritual journeys," he announced. His eyes sparkled behind the little glasses and for a moment he became much more animated, carried away no doubt by enthusiasm for the job.

"Spiritual journeys?" I repeated, a bit doubtfully. I had visions of a week in a monastic retreat or a course on art history, neither of which appealed. If I wanted boredom I could get it any day of the week at Lorder's.

"Yes," he said, positively gushing with enthusiasm. "For the truly sensitive, the truly open-minded individual, we offer a range of unique supernatural experiences."

"Supernatural?" I gaped at him for a moment before I remembered to shut my mouth.

"Oh, yes," he went on. "For those who have ever wondered whether there really *is* anything out there— whether life continues after we have shuffled off this mortal coil—or for those who simply wish to experience the ultimate frisson that only comes from a close encounter with the world beyond, Von Teufel Travel offers a unique opportunity to find out." And he went on a bit more like that, whilst I digested what he had just said. Of course it had to be a gimmick, though it was a new one, I'd give him that. Furthermore, he'd got himself a good audience this time. Not a lot of people know this (not even my sister, bless her), but I'm quite an avid reader of what they call *genre* fiction, in my spare time. Call it my private vice, if you like. Where other fellows like to peruse the sports pages of the *Telegraph* or even read rags like *Playboy* (like Watson, for example, I shouldn't wonder), well, I like to curl up with a good horror novel. It takes me out of myself, as they say. So one way and another I quite enjoyed Cornelius Von Teufel's little performance, and of course I decided to enter into the spirit of it.

"Well, let me see what you can offer," I said gamely.

"Ah, a true connoisseur," he beamed. "Step this way, if you would, please."

We went towards the back of the shop where there was a little area that looked more like a gentleman's club than anything—all green leather chairs, sporting prints on the walls and an expensive-looking Persian rug. I sat in one of the chairs and he fussed around gathering papers together. Eventually he sat in a chair opposite me and perused the uppermost sheet over the top of his spectacles.

"Many of our clients enjoy the more traditional trips," he began. "I can offer you the *Bram Stoker Special*, which comprises a five day tour of Transylvania, including Castle

Dracula, and ends with a visit to the Lair of the White Worm. Very popular, especially with vermologists."

I shuddered. "Not really my cup of tea."

"Alternatively," he went on undaunted, "we can offer music lovers the chance to experience the beautiful city of Paris with the *Gaston Leroux Phantom Deluxe*."

"Music lovers?" I repeated, visions of the Moulin Rouge rising enticingly before my eyes.

"Opera, of course," he remarked in his quiet voice.

Opera! Fat women with hordes of chins screeching away in Viking helmets! Hastily I held up my hand. "No, thank you. Not," I continued, seeing one of those neat eyebrows rising slightly, "that I have anything against culture."

"Then perhaps you would enjoy our *Haywain* trip," suggested Von Teufel. "An opportunity to literally step into the mind of the artist."

"Haywain?" I said. "Isn't that by Constable? The one with the horses and the river? Pardon me for saying so, but I don't see anything particularly supernatural about that."

"Ah yes, a number of people have made that assumption," he said. "The name actually refers to the *Haywain* by Hieronymus Bosch." He fell silent for a moment, reflecting. "I rather think we must change the name of that particular trip; there have been *complaints*. I recall one elderly gentleman explicitly objected to the impaling. Some people have, I fear, very little appreciation for mediaeval symbolism."

"Look here," I said, "I'm sure impaling and gigantic worms are all very well in their place, but I'm really looking for something a little more subtle. This is supposed to be a holiday after all—don't you have anything with just a *suggestion* of nastiness, rather than going the whole hog?"

To give him his due, Von Teufel took this on the chin. "Absolutely," he said very smoothly, without any sign of offence. "For those who prefer a more understated apparition, I would thoroughly recommend the *M.R. James Memorial Trip to Burnstow.*"

This sounded a lot more interesting. I sat forward. "What does that involve?" I asked hopefully.

"First class travel to and from Burnstow, a tour of the beach and a visit to the Green Dragon," he informed me.

"Well, that sounds excellent," I said, starting to feel quite enthusiastic. Then a thought struck me. "Hang on, I don't remember any Green Dragon," I said. "Wasn't it the Globe Inn in the story?"

He had the grace to look a little ashamed. "Indeed it was, Mr. Larkin; you are quite right."

"So what's the Green Dragon, then?"

"It's a top quality launderette," he admitted. "There is a good deal of crumpled linen," he added.

"It's not really the same, though, is it?" I remarked. "Why can't I visit the Globe instead?"

"Alas, not possible," he said, spreading his hands in a gesture of regret. "It burnt to the ground some years ago. A fire in the linen cupboard, I believe. Some guests were charged, but I don't believe it came to anything."

I sighed. "I'm very sorry, but none of these really appeals. Is there really nothing else you can offer me?"

"Well," he replied slowly, as though debating whether to commit himself, "For particular very valued customers we do offer a self catering option."

"Self catering?" I said. "You mean, I would stay in a haunted house? Can you absolutely guarantee it would be haunted?"

"Oh yes," he said with enthusiasm. He looked straight at me and I saw his eyes twinkling behind his steel-rimmed glasses. "It would be a hundred per cent guaranteed to be haunted."

"Wonderful," I said. "Can you show me some properties?"

"Of course." He arose and fetched a thick file, which he spread on an occasional table before me. "We have a range of properties including period houses, several castles, an old mill and a lighthouse."

I leaned over and peered at the pictures. "What about this?" I asked. "Borley Rectory—I've heard of that one."

"Alas, fully booked for the foreseeable future," said Von Teufel. "But if you would prefer an ecclesiastical environment, we have a very nice vicarage in Hampshire."

"Well, let's take a look," I said, thinking that it would be very convenient if I wanted to run down and see my sister for the day. I perused the photograph. It was a very attractive property—Queen Anne, I think they call it, with red bricks and white windows. "I see it has four bedrooms," I commented, running my eye down the information printed underneath the photo.

"Yes, indeed," said Von Teufel quietly. He looked at me, meditatively. "For you, Mr. Larkin, I think I would suggest the *blue* bedroom."

I won't bore you with the discussion about possible dates and all the rest of it. Eventually I got out my little-used credit card and paid a sizeable deposit to Von Teufel Travel, and then I signed a contract. Of course, you will say I should have read the small print, but Von Teufel seemed such a gentleman I felt it would be pointedly impolite to give him the third degree about the details. The only thing I did think was a bit funny at the time was that the contract was all written in red ink, but I thought perhaps that was something to do with travel regulations. Anyway, I signed with a flourish, and was just straightening up when Von Teufel came up close to me with something glittering in his hand. I took it for a silver fountain pen, thinking he was going to add his own name to the contract or something. You will think me dreadfully naïve, but I didn't even smell a rat when he asked me to stand up a little straighter. Obligingly I did so, and with one wonderfully swift movement he flourished the glittering object aloft then plunged it into my chest. You know, they say it is remarkably difficult to stab someone in the heart, regardless of what might occur in popular fiction; the organ is well protected in its cage of ribs, and genuine stabs to the heart are usually the result of luck rather than judgement. All I can say on this point is that Cornelius Von Teufel was either very lucky or extremely skilful in his aim. The side of the blade scraped a little against one rib, I'll grant you that, but otherwise his aim was true, and the knife slid into my heart and punctured it like a balloon. It is a very curious experience, I can tell you, to feel one's heart skewered like a piece of barbecue meat. Instantly I felt the front of my shirt grow hot and wet, but after that I felt very little, for the room was growing dim and faint around me. I could feel my heart making one last sad attempt to beat, and the blood came pumping out over my hands and pattered down onto my shoes. I tottered on my feet, and Cornelius Von Teufel laid a steadying hand on my shoulder. As at last I drifted away into blackness, I heard his soft voice say, "*Bon voyage*." That puzzled me a bit—I could have sworn he was German.

So here I am, in the blue room, on what you might call an extended holiday. At any rate, I have plenty of spare time, and my asthma no longer bothers me—no lungs, you see. The vicarage isn't inhabited by the Living just at present, but I'm not lonely. I have company.

One of the things that you may not know if you have not yet crossed the Great Divide, is that the Recently Deceased do have a certain amount of influence—especially those who have died a violent death. It is comparatively short-lived, which is why so many apparitions have to vent their wrath through groaning and clanking and other ineffectual activities; but for a short time the influence is relatively powerful. In Death I like to think I demonstrated a little more drive than I ever did in Life, working at Lorder's. What I did was this: I encouraged Watson to take a holiday too.

I think he should be grateful really: actual Death couldn't possibly be any worse than working at Lorder's for another thirty years. But all the same, he never stops complaining. The trouble with Watson is that he is terribly vain. And there's no doubt his looks have changed a little, and not for the better. Cornelius Von Teufel stabbed him twice, you see—through the eyes. And it's hard to look debonair if your eyes look like two overcooked tomatoes that someone has punctured with a kebab skewer. Still, he's stuck with them now; and as I said at the beginning, he's only himself to blame.

Nathair Dhubh

What? Oh yes, yes, please do sit down. Crowded in here tonight, isn't it? No, no, you're not disturbing me. I'm not waiting for anyone. The only person I'd be likely to drink with in here was my pal Tom, and I'm not expecting *him* tonight. Climbers, are you? Thought so. Did a bit of climbing myself once. No more, though. That was before the last War. We didn't have any of these fancy ballet shoes that you youngsters wear these days. And all this ironmongery you carry around! Boots we had, with bloody great nails on the bottom of them, and a rope. That was it.

Thank you—don't mind if I do. A pint of eighty shilling.

So, where were you climbing today, then, lads? Yes, I know it. Well, if you were up there early you'll have had a fine view before this rain came in. Been up a few routes there myself a long time ago, though it didn't have any of these names to it then. What did you say that last one was called? Ridiculous . . . !

Well, I did my bit of climbing before the War. Last climb I did was a way from here, back in September '38. I'm a long way the wrong side of eighty now, but I can remember it like it was yesterday. Never climbed again after that. Never had the heart for it. Why? If you really want to know the answer to that, I'll tell you, only sit at peace—and when I'm done don't pester me with questions. I'll tell you the truth as I saw it, and for the rest, I've no more idea than you have. This is what happened.

I was born this side of the border, but I lived away for much of my working life, as you can maybe tell from my voice. I was born and raised in a place some miles north of here, and that's all I'm saying about that. It was a smallish town, not much more than a village really, and remote even for those days. This was between the Wars. There wasn't much to do for young lads in such a place, so when we weren't working, me and my pal Tom, we used to go off up into the hills and climb a few crags. My mother, God rest her, had had my little sister Lou, who died a young girl in 1946, so she was pretty occupied with her. Tom had no mother, she'd been dead some years, only his father, who was a bit handy with his fists. So one way and another, no-one much missed us if we went off. We'd sit up on the top of some crag and look down at the town and plan how we were going to get away and make our fortunes. Well, I got out, but Tom never did.

Now, this particular morning, the ninth of September it was, Tom was supposed to be working in his father's place, but it came up so clear and fresh and dry it was a sin to be indoors all day. I guess he thought this too, for I was finishing my breakfast when the front door of our house opened and in came Tom with a rope slung over his shoulder.

"Come on, Jim," he says. "It's a fine day for climbing."

"Aren't you supposed to be working for the old man this morning, Tom?" I asked him.

"Bother the old man," replied Tom. Altogether there was an air about him this morning, like he was a bit excited about something, looking forward to it or afeard of it, I'm not sure which. You could always tell when he was up to something. He had a bit of the devil in him sometimes, had Tom. Anyway he comes up to the table and leans right over to me, his eyes sort of glittering with the excitement and he says, "I've a mind to climb Nathair Dhubh."

Well, this was unexpected, not to say unwelcome, and I took a couple of swallows of tea to give myself time to think about what to say to this. Now, Nathair Dhubh, that was the local name of a particular crag, and a peculiar one it was too. I'm not sure what you'd call it as rock formations go, a pinnacle or a stack or some suchlike. Anyway it stuck up out of the other rocks around it for all the world like a cobra snake rearing up to strike. Maybe that's how it got its local name, for *nathair* means snake, and *dhubh*, as you know, means black. Or there may have been other reasons, but I'll come to those in a minute. Anyway, this Nathair Dhubh was sure to be a horror of a climb; only one side was really accessible at all, the back of it being sheer and featureless like a wall. These days you might get up it with those boots with the sticky soles but remember, in those days we were climbing with big leather boots with nails underneath, and what's more we didn't have any of these bits of ironmongery that you can use to protect yourself with now. We didn't have pitons or runners or any of that, either—we were just two lads messing about with a rope and the rule was, the one who went up first just didn't fall off. So the back of Nathair Dhubh was out. The front wasn't much better, but at least there were a few features. The first bit wasn't too bad, though it made a fair few feet of height, but then there was a piece of rock jutting right out to make an overhang. A little further up, about the height of a man's head if he were standing on top of the first overhang, was another bulge of rock, so that if you looked at the whole thing from the side it was like the open jaws of the snake. Once you'd got past that there was another climb up to the very top, but it was impossible to tell from the bottom or from the surrounding outcrops exactly what that last bit was like.

Now you'll no doubt be thinking that the reason I didn't fancy the climb was that I was afraid of it or didn't trust my own climbing. Well, it was another reason than that. Nathair Dhubh had a reputation amongst the local folk. No, nothing as solid as a ghost story or any such thing. It just seemed to have a sort of repulsion for them, especially the older ones. Certainly no-one would have thought of climbing up it even if it were not so blessed steep, but not only that, no-one liked to walk along the bit of land underneath it, and in some indefinable way it was unlucky even to look straight at it. People just ignored it most of the time. The only thing I ever heard anyone say about it, and that was my granny, when she was older than I am now, was that Nathair Dhubh was named for that old serpent which is mentioned in Revelation.

It's no use asking me questions about the Nathair Dhubh. I wouldn't tell you lads where it was even if it were still standing, which it isn't, as I heard long after that it fell down in the seventies, a huge chunk of it just sheared off and came down.

Well, there was Tom with his rope, and as I gulped down my last mouthful of hot tea he said, all eagerly, "Are you coming?" with his eyes all alight with the excitement of it. He was like that, he had this devil-may-care streak and somehow I always got caught up with it. I suppose you might say I was easily led in those days, but it was exciting to be led by Tom. He didn't give a monkey's about anything except being outdoors, and he could climb like fury, and he had such a passion for it that I couldn't help getting caught up in it myself.

So rather against my better judgement I said, "Yes" and went off to get my boots whilst Tom picked over the remains of my breakfast and stuffed his mouth with cold toast.

Well, off we went. It was a longish walk in to that part of the hills where the Nathair Dhubh was, but the morning was fresh and clear. For the first part of the walk in we followed a farm track, then turning off that we went up a shepherd's path for a mile or two more. After that we were off any path altogether, and the ground got rougher underfoot, with stones and scrubby bits of plants. As we gained height we went a little slower and Tom shifted the rope to his other shoulder. I remember we went alongside a little stream for a half mile or so. Just where it came down over some stones, Tom saw something white in the water. Rolling up his sleeve he fished it out, but it was just the jawbone of a sheep, the teeth still sticking out of it, and he threw it down again.

By the time we reached the higher ground under the Nathair Dhubh, it was late morning and as bright as you could wish for—not a cloud in sight, the sort of day that's a gift to anyone who loves to be up in the hills. I could feel my spirits rising. It was exhilarating being up there, with the breeze and the great wide open blue sky and the crags jutting up into it, and the prospect of a totally new climb. And make no mistake about it—I was itching for that climb. Any reluctance I'd felt earlier had all melted away. I could feel my fingers flexing as I looked up at the outline of Nathair Dhubh, as though they were already feeling for the holds. It was Tom's climb though—he was to lead, no discussion needed and no words spoken. He'd already checked the rope over and was tying it around himself. He looked at me and he was grinning like a loon. Couldn't wait to get off the ground, he couldn't.

Well, we had a look at the first ten feet or so of the rock and it was pretty clear which way he was going to have to go up; the right side of it had far better holds than the left side where you'd have had to jump up to get onto anything, and even then you'd have had a job to hold on. I'd have to say it wasn't a particularly difficult climb up until you got to that first overhang, but it had the merit that it had never been climbed before, and the added attraction that everyone would say we shouldn't have done it when we got down afterwards. We reckoned it would be a single pitch—couldn't tell you what grade it would have been though. Maybe you lads would make light work of it with your modern boots and whatnot—and maybe not.

So I took the other end of the rope, leaving Tom a good bit of slack, and he started off up the climb. He got up the first few feet all right, until he was just above the height of my head, and then it was obviously harder than it looked, as he slowed down a bit and started feeling about the holds, trying to get a decent grip. He missed his footing once and I saw the light glint on the nails on the bottom of his boot as his foot swung out from the rock. Then he got his foot back onto a more substantial hold and he was up another couple of feet. I went on paying out the rope, but I was getting a crick in my neck from looking upwards, so I put my head down for a moment and moved it from side to side, trying to get the ache out of it. I glanced downhill and everything was as peaceful as you can imagine, dead quiet in fact, with the September sun beating down on the stones and not so much as a sheep in sight. When I looked up again a moment later, Tom was just under the overhang. If that overhang had run the width of the crag, I reckon he never would've got up it, considering we didn't have any protection, but just over at the right of it there was a narrow place at the corner where the overhang ran into the rock face and you could hoist yourself up and round, if you didn't mind being a bit exposed. I could see Tom's lips moving and guessed he was cussing to himself, but he eventually managed it and a minute later he was standing up on that first overhang, looking like Lord Nelson standing on the poopdeck admiring his fleet. I shouted up a bit of abuse to that effect, but he didn't take any notice. After a moment he turned and started examining the rock in front of him, working out the best route to the next overhang, which was however not quite as tricky as the first one, having a good solid hold at the side to hang onto. It didn't take him long before he was heaving himself over that next outcrop, and then he disappeared from view and the rope slithered up after him. Well, I stood there looking up and my stomach was starting to turn over a little, as I knew it wouldn't be long before he got to the top, and then it'd be my turn to climb up and wrestle my way past those blessed overhangs. I wasn't afraid, but the thought of it got my blood up and the sooner I got onto that climb the better, I reckoned

Anyway, it's best to keep your wits about you even when you're seconding, as you know, in case the leader decides to take a tumble and flatten anyone underneath. But in spite of this, something made me take my eye off the rock above and glance round behind me again. Then I saw something I didn't like at all. No, not at all. There was a mist coming in.

Now, you know as well as I do how fast the mist can come in in these parts. But you don't expect to see it at midday when the whole morning has been as clear and as dry as you like, not a cloud in sight and the sun still shining overhead. And what's more, there was something I didn't care for about this mist. For one thing, it was moving in pretty fast, like a strong breeze was bringing it along the side of the hill towards me, but I couldn't feel any movement in the air. And it was thick white, so you couldn't see a thing in it. Altogether there was something not right about it, and it struck me that I had no fancy at all for climbing around on the Nathair Dhubh in it.

So I stepped back a bit from the rock and hollered, "*Tom!*" at the top of my voice, peering up at that topmost overhang where I'd last seen him. A second or two later I saw his head appear over the outcrop of rock. I think he called something back, but whatever it was, the words were lost. I called his name again and pointed at the mist, and I saw his head turn to look at it. Then he disappeared from view again.

To tell you the truth, this was a bit of a fix, as we couldn't have foreseen this happening and we hadn't made any plan for it. Nor did I have any idea what the top of the crag was like or how difficult it was to get onto. Either Tom could make for the top of it, or he could try to find something to belay onto where he was. But would he wait for me to come up in spite of the mist, or would he lower himself down right away? One thing was for sure, we weren't going to have a discussion about this, since I hadn't heard a word of what he'd shouted down the last time. Then, whilst I was standing there thinking about it, up came the mist and the next second it had engulfed me.

Well, it was a real pea-souper, the like of which I'd never seen before and have never seen since, thank God. I could see the rock, and my hands on the rope before me, but not much else. It was chilly and it seemed to deaden sound so that all I could hear was my own breathing. Then an idea came over me which seemed to strike my blood cold in my veins and make my stomach turn right over, that this wasn't a mist at all but the *serpent's breath*. I stood there in the whiteness with the hairs rising on the back of my neck. And then I felt a light tug on my hands as the rope started paying out again.

Well, there's been a lot said about the Character of Men in recent times, and not much of it complimentary, but I'm telling you there's times when a bit of the fighting spirit and not wanting to lose your face in front of another bloke can be the only thing that keeps you from a total funk. Part of me wanted to drop that rope and go haring off down that hill as fast as my legs would carry me, but I couldn't think how I'd face Tom afterwards. And you know, there's a brotherhood amongst climbers, and it would've been an unforgiveable thing to leave him, like abandoning your mate on a battlefield. So there I stood, but I was only just holding it together. All round me was white, white and more white, and that deathly chill in the air, and the only thing that moved was the rope as it paid out almost to the very end.

At last it stopped moving, and the bit of slack that hung between me and the rock swayed very lightly in the air with a sort of expectant look about it, like it was waiting for me to do something.

I stepped up close to the rock and laid my hand on it, and whether it was the mist in the air I don't know, but it felt a little bit damp under my fingers in not at all a pleasant way. So I stepped back again, and feeling self-conscious like you might if you started bellowing your lungs out in a churchyard, I put my head back and bawled out Tom's name a couple of times. Then I listened, but I couldn't hear a thing, for the mist had deadened all sound. I waited for a very long time, and then I gave a very gentle tug on the rope, not liking to yank on it too much in case Tom hadn't reached a belay point. Then I waited again. There was no answering tug on the rope, and still no sound at all from above.

Well, I ask you, lads, what would *you* have done? There was nothing to see, no sound or movement from above, no sign whether Tom was still going up or coming down, or anything. If I climbed up and he hadn't got to the top and set up a belay, I wouldn't have any protection if I fell, and I'd probably pull him off the rock too. On the other hand, he might be sitting up there freezing half to death and cursing me in every direction for not getting a move on. I waited, and I waited, and I waited. It seemed like an hour had passed and still there was no sign from above. I was getting a real chill in my fingers and I realised that if I were going to climb that crag it was going to have to be now, before I got too bally cold to hold on. Well, our signal for the second to climb was two tugs on the rope, so I tugged on it twice, a bit gingerly, and then I started to climb Nathair Dhubh.

To look at me these days with these gnarled-up old hands and this stick, you wouldn't think I'd ever have been much of a climber, but I'm telling you, for those days I was pretty fair, for all that I was a bit more careful than Tom was. But all the same, I had a struggle on the first bit of that climb. I couldn't think how Tom had got up it so easy. Those holds he'd got his fingers round so nicely didn't seem so good at all to me. Either they stuck out less than they'd seemed to before, or they sloped downwards a bit so you didn't feel secure standing on them, not with those old-fashioned boots anyway. And some of them were downright jagged, so it hurt your fingers to hold on to them. You couldn't stand there and rest whilst you thought about your next move—it was onwards and upwards or down again the quick way. Well, some climbs you have to fight with more than others, but I'll tell you, the only way I got up this one was brute strength and ignorance. At last I hauled myself up onto that first ledge and lay there like a grounded fish.

And what of Tom all this time, you ask? Well, I'd still not heard a sound from above, but whilst I was cursing and heaving myself up that first bit of rock, I'd felt the rope take in a little, so I was hoping he'd belayed at the top, not that I was planning to fall off and try him. Now whilst I was lying on that overhang catching my breath, the rope took in some more until it was tight, and I was getting a slight bit of encouragement to stand up and get on with the climbing. So up I got, feeling irritated with Tom, and was just opening my mouth to yell up and ask him why he couldn't let a chap climb in his own good time, when the rope took in quickly and hard and almost jerked me face-first into the rock. I let fly with some ripe language at that, but I started to climb again anyway, reckoning I might as well get the whole sorry experience over and done with.

Well, now I seemed to get on better, whether it was that the climb got a bit easier or I was getting into my stride, I can't say. I was up that next stretch to the second overhang like a monkey, and all the time the rope was taken in very smoothly, so there was always that little bit of tension on it. I paused for a moment whilst I was getting ready to make the reach up onto the hold by the ledge and swing myself up onto it, and I could feel a very slight pull on the rope. Then a thought occurred to me, and not a pleasant one.

You know when a rope's being taken in, there's a very slight rhythm to it, from your partner's taking in one hand's reach after another? Well, I couldn't feel that at all. It felt as though the rope was being taken in in one smooth motion, just as though I were a fish being reeled in on the end of a line. And now I'd paused, you could feel it tugging just a little, like it was trying to urge me on upwards. Well, I climbed. Nothing else for it—I was committed, and if there was monkey business going on, like I was beginning to suspect, the sooner I got to the top and squared up to it, the better. I cussed Tom a bit under my breath, more to keep my spirits up than anything, like whistling in the dark, and I kept on moving up that rock. I got past the second overhang all right, and now, I thought, I must be on the last stretch before the top, though I couldn't see much above or below me for the mist.

"*Tom!*" I yelled. Surely he must be able to hear me by now? But there was never a sound from above. I could see an edge above me, and white mist above that, so this must be the top of the crag, the top of Nathair Dhubh. Now the rope was taking in a little more rapidly, there was a bit of a pull on it, and I was scrambling up the rock faster than I'd have liked to. I was breathing hard, my heart was thumping and the blood was roaring in my ears, but the pull up that rock wasn't coming from me, it wasn't even coming from that blasted rope tugging at me, it was coming from somewhere outside me. It was like the rock itself was pulling me on upwards; there was a sort of *eagerness* which filled the air, like the Nathair Dhubh itself was calling me on up there. Up the last few feet I went like a wild thing, and a proper sight I must have made, wide-eyed and heaving and panting and my fingers all scraped and bloody in places.

Well, I hauled myself at last onto the top of that blasted crag, and do you know, at that very selfsame instant the mist just ebbed away—rolled back like a tide it did, and the midday sunshine suddenly streaming down just about blinded me. I put up an arm to shield my eyes from that dazzling sun, and the next moment I realised that I was alone.

Not a mortal soul was there on that rock apart from me.

For a few seconds I stood there blinking and looking around me like a man dazed, for my brain wouldn't take in what my eyes were telling it. There I was on the top of the rock, with a drop on every side; there was room enough for three or four to sit up there if they liked, but there was nowhere anyone could hide. All the same, for those first few moments I kept on looking and looking, as if I would see Tom if I only looked hard enough. Then at last I looked down and saw the rope. That gave me a start, I can tell you. There it lay all spilled out over the rock; you could see the coils lying there loosely, like someone had been winding it in quite neatly, but had then just dropped the rope on the ground. One end of course was still tied around me, but the other end I could see just lying there on the rock, not attached to anything at all. Well, I felt a bit sick at that, and what with the sun beating down on my head, and the empty air all around, and me so high up there that the town away down in the distance looked just like a child's toy, I felt like I was going to pass out, and I sat down quick on the rock. Still I couldn't get it out of my head that Tom must be up here somewhere. So after a while, when my head had cleared a little, I got up cautiously and went right round the top of the Nathair Dhubh, looking down every side. Not hair nor hide of Tom did I find on any side. I looked down the back of the crag where it was all smooth like a wall, and I knew for certain that he couldn't have gone down there without a rope, not unless he'd fallen, in which case he'd have been all in smithereens at the bottom. The sides weren't much better, and I'd come up the front face myself. As far as I could see, there only was one route which was climbable, and I'd come up it.

Still, I didn't like to think he'd just vanished into thin air, it didn't seem rational, so next I scanned the hillside and the rocks all around, just in case I should spot him somewhere, but everything was absolutely still and deserted. There weren't even any plants growing up there; there was no vegetation to move in the breeze, and not so much as a bird hopping around amongst those stones. Well, I sat there for a while, not knowing what to do next, and thinking maybe that if I kept an eye on the ground below I'd see Tom come out from behind a rock with a big grin on his face and call up to tell me what a fool I'd been. I think all the time I realised that there was no way he could have got down that rock without me knowing, but my mind couldn't seem to get a grip on the thought, so there I sat and waited, feeling strangely passive.

At last I could see that the shadows were starting to lengthen and it was getting well on in the afternoon, so if I were going to get down the Nathair Dhubh before evening I would have to do it by myself. In spite of the inertia that seemed to have come over me, I could still feel an uncomfortable prickle of fear when I thought about evening coming, and then the night. So I set up a belay round a big chunk of rock and made ready to lower myself off the crag. I kept looking around me, still thinking that Tom might suddenly spring out of somewhere, but all was dead quiet, and I lowered myself off the edge and down to the ground below without incident.

It was a sad walk I had, trudging back down to the town on my own. Once I looked back to see if I could see a figure anywhere amongst the rocks, but nothing moved there and I was sick of the sight of Nathair Dhubh brooding above me. I went on my way and didn't look back again.

When I got home, my sister Lou had been taken ill and my mother was fussing round her with blankets and warm milk and suchlike, so she didn't take much notice as I came in. A good thing too, for when I caught sight of myself in the mirror on the upstairs landing, I'd a face as drawn and white as a corpse's. I went into my room and sat on my bed to think. I didn't like to tell anyone what had happened, not yet; I knew there'd be trouble when they found out where we'd been. Anyway, I told myself, Tom was probably messing about; he'd be round here in the morning laughing at me for a gullible idiot, and right silly I'd look if I'd called out half the town searching for him. In the end I decided I would wait until the morning, and if he still hadn't shown up, well, I'd have to organise a search party.

I can see by your faces you think this was the wrong idea. Of course, if he'd have been lying amongst the rocks there with a broken leg or something, the sooner we got him back the better; you wouldn't reckon his chances if he'd been out there all night. But I was pretty sure I knew what reaction I'd get if I asked anyone to come up to the Nathair Dhubh with me to look for him, what with the evening coming in. They'd be mad as hell and say we were a pair of silly young fools wasting our time climbing around places that were best left to the birds and the sheep, and Tom's dad would be worse, he'd be looking for someone to thump. But this was only half the story; you see, the main reason I never said anything that night was that I knew in my heart that it wasn't any use.

Well, I had a bad night of it, with dreams that I couldn't remember when I woke up, but which left me with a terrible feeling of emptiness. I tossed and turned all night, and when I got up next morning I felt hardly any better than I did when I lay down. So I went out early before breakfast, down to Tom's house, and knocked on the door. It took his old man a long time to answer, and when he did, he looked pretty rough, leaning on the doorframe and blinking like a mole in the cold early sunlight. I reckon he must have been feeling very bad because although he was pretty short with me he couldn't be bothered to let me have it for waking him up so early. No, he said, Tom hadn't come in the night before, and if I saw him I could damn well tell him where to go. As I turned and walked off I heard the door slam shut again.

At last, round about midday, I managed to get together a small search party to come up to the Nathair Dhubh with me and look for Tom. Of course we never found a thing. We went round and round that rock and never found so much as a brass button, nor did we find any sign of him anywhere in the land thereabouts. We came back in low spirits, glad to be out of the shadow of the Nathair Dhubh, and with the others complaining about being taken on a wild goose chase. When Tom hadn't come back by nightfall that day, or the next day, or the day after that, folks had to take his disappearance seriously, but most of them concluded that he'd got fed up with fighting with his old man and taken off somewhere. The next year the War broke out, and with so many young lives lost, no-one ever gave much of a thought to young Tom disappearing like that. Well, who knows, if he had taken off somehow, he could have signed up, wherever he'd gone, and maybe he was just more grist to the mill like the rest of my generation. But I don't think so, and so far as I know, his name's not on any memorial.

And me? I never climbed again after that. Of course I never went anywhere near the Nathair Dhubh again after that September, and after the War I moved away from the town. But it wasn't just the place, you know; Nathair Dhubh had spoiled climbing for me for good and all. I never could bear the thought anymore of standing at the bottom of a crag waiting for the signal to climb. Standing there on my own, not knowing what I'd find when I got to the top. Well, could *you*?

Alberic de Mauléon

On a certain hot afternoon in June of 1682, a band of richly-dressed horsemen bearing the livery of Mauléon rode up through the narrow streets of Saint Bertrand de Comminges and clattered into the paved square before the great cathedral of Sainte-Marie. In the reign of the *Roi-Soleil,* when the coming of the *Sans-Culottes* and the burning of the chapter library lay a full hundred years in the future, Saint Bertrand was a prosperous town, and yet the attire of the visitors was opulent enough to attract attention. A group of ragged urchins ran barefoot alongside the horses, begging for a *denier,* and not a few of the townspeople appeared on the doorsteps of their stone houses, to watch the wealthy strangers ride by.

The riders reined in before the west door of the cathedral, the iron of the horses' shoes ringing out as they pranced upon the stone pavement. The foremost of the riders, and the most ostentatiously dressed, rode right up to the cathedral entrance on his glossy black horse and uttered a single word in ringing tones.

"Alberic!"

When his cry elicited no response, he repeated it, not once, but three times. Seeing that the door remained resolutely closed to him, he barked a command to his companions, two of whom dismounted and approached the door.

Before they had time to pound upon it with their gloved fists, however, it opened from within, and a single figure appeared framed within the doorway. His sober, dark ecclesiastical costume could not entirely obscure the grace and symmetry of his form; in truth, Canon Alberic de Mauléon was a handsome fellow, let him try as hard as he might to conceal this fact under rough wool and an earnest expression. He was a man of perhaps twenty-five summers, with strong features, clear dark eyes and glossy black hair which he cut short in repudiation of fashion. This was not, however, the most remarkable thing about him—what was striking was the resemblance he bore to the splendidly attired horseman who had called his name. But for the fact that the rider wore a magnificent curled wig, and his colour was heightened from his exertions, the two men were identical. As the Canon gazed upon the newcomer, he might have been staring into a mirror.

"Brother," he said at last in a neutral tone. "Henri. What brings you here?"

"News," said Henri de Mauléon. "I have news. Will you hear it?"

"Will you do me the favour of dismounting?" asked Canon Alberic, eyeing the iron-shod hooves of his brother's horse as they danced unnervingly close to him. He stood his ground, but then the animal suddenly moved forward, and he was forced to step smartly backwards. A book that he had been holding under his arm slipped from his grasp onto the pavement, spilling a handful of loose leaves as it did so. With an exclamation, Canon Alberic made as if to gather them up, but the horse was now prancing so restlessly that he was forced to abandon the attempt.

Henri de Mauléon seemed not displeased by this turn of events. However, he swung himself down from the saddle and handed the reins to one of his attendants.

"Still indulging your passion for sketching, Alberic?" he asked in a mocking tone, plucking one of the papers from the pavement. "You had better spend your time performing good works and kissing the bishop's arse."

The drawing he held in his gloved hand was well-executed, a finely-detailed depiction of a miser grasping a bulging money-bag, disappearing down the gaping gullet of a monster. Had Henri de Mauléon been familiar with the cathedral of Sainte-Marie, or had he taken the time to study the carved doorframe not a dozen paces from where he stood, he might have recognised the subject as one of the stone ornaments.

"What is this, brother? My Lord Bishop taking his dinner?"

"It is a rich man being consumed by a devil," responded the Canon. His voice was even but for the first time the blood came to his face. Not a murmur escaped his lips as his twin crumpled the drawing into a ball and let it fall upon the paving-stones, but his eyes followed the boot-heel which ground it into fragments.

Henri de Mauléon thrust his face close to his brother's. "Folly," he retorted. "The rich man could so easily have been *you*, brother Alberic, were it not for an accident of birth. A very small accident . . . only minutes." He smiled unpleasantly. "If you had pushed yourself forward, Alberic, as you are so loath to do, you might be the heir of Mauléon, and I the obscure, struggling priest with a useless longing for the arts."

"You would make a very poor canon," observed Alberic quietly. He folded his hands and looked his brother in the eyes. "You said that you have news for me."

"Ha! Indeed I do." Henri's manner, ever mercurial, was suddenly jovial, but its apparent warmth failed to infect his brother. Experience taught that when the heir of Mauléon was in so good a humour it rarely meant anything welcome for anyone else. Now Henri took off his glove and extended his hand to his brother. "Congratulate me, brother. I am to marry."

Canon Alberic regarded the outstretched hand dubiously, but there was nothing to do but take it. He put out his own hand with the air of a man about to undergo the trial by hot iron.

"May I ask, who is the lady?" he enquired.

"The fair and very virtuous *Demoiselle* Isabelle Rouvignac," declared Henri de Mauléon. As he spoke the words, his gaze never left his brother's face.

The Canon was visibly struck as though by a physical blow. His face a blank mask of shock, he took a step back, releasing his brother's hand as though he had been stung. With a supreme effort he maintained his self-control, suppressing the desire to seize his twin by the throat and throttle him until the savage smile of triumph on his face turned black with choking. Still his hands with their slender fingers contracted into fists.

Henri drank in all this like a glutton who has gorged himself at a banquet and was still unable to resist taking the last morsel from under the nose of a watching pauper.

"Will you not congratulate me, Alberic?" he asked mockingly. "Well, perhaps not. A man who has chosen to dedicate his life to the church can have no thought of the pleasures of earthly love."

"Chosen?" repeated the Canon in a low tone of rigidly suppressed fury.

Henri gave a short ugly bark of laughter. "Well, chosen in as much as the younger brother, the nobody with no fortune, can choose anything for himself, *n'est-ce pas*?" He nodded to his attendants and swung himself back into the saddle of his horse. "I bid you good-day, brother. Attend the wedding or not, as you wish."

Canon Alberic watched unmoving as Henri de Mauléon and his retinue trotted back across the sun-drenched square. Even after they had turned the corner and vanished down one of the narrow streets, the clatter of iron-shod hooves and the sound of voices were audible for several minutes.

The Canon stood and listened until the sound had died away altogether. Then he knelt and gathered up the remaining leaves that had fluttered from his book, moving with such icy calm that he might have been going about his devotional duties in the cathedral. When he had finished, he walked back to the door and vanished into the gloom within. If his burden had become heavier, if he staggered under the weight of his affliction, he did not show it.

The month of February 1694 was a cruelly cold one. The lone visitor who arrived on horseback at the Château de Mauléon was half-frozen, the shoulders of his greatcoat frosted white by the falling snow. When the waiting servants had taken his horse, Canon Alberic entered the château by the main door, passing under the arms of Mauléon that were carved into the grey stone. He did not pause to regard with any affectionate nostalgia the weathered lion rampant, nor did he enter with any sense of homecoming.

Henri de Mauléon, alerted to his arrival by the boom of the great door closing against the wind, descended the stone staircase to meet his brother, and for a moment the two men looked at each other in silence.

The years had been good to both of them. Henri still wore a magnificent wig, his brother his own hair, and there was but little hoar-frost in the dark locks that clustered about the Canon's temples. Henri's figure was the more robust, upholstered by years of good eating and luxury, whereas the Canon remained lean and ascetic, but still a stranger might have taken one for the other.

"You heeded my summons," said Henri de Mauléon, not bothering to greet his brother nor attempt to embrace him.

"I would have come for no other earthly reason than the one you gave me," retorted Canon Alberic.

"You are passionate, Alberic," said Henri scornfully. "You are a fool." He shrugged his shoulders. "Yet it seems you are the only fool she will see. She has sent her chaplain away; if you do not go to her she will die unconfessed."

"Then take me to her," said the Canon bluntly. He bowed his head and followed his brother up the stone staircase.

The chamber to which Henri brought him lay at the back of the château overlooking the gardens, but at present the heavy brocade drapes were tightly closed, so that the room required the illumination of candles. A fire was burning in the hearth and the chamber was unpleasantly hot. Henri did not linger, and Canon Alberic did not look around for him. He approached the high-canopied bed and its dying occupant in the guise of a cleric, but his man's soul was on his lips.

"Isabelle," he said softly.

The face on the pillow turned to him and he saw with a shock of recognition that she was still the same. The twelve years that had passed had not robbed her of her beauty, although her features were thinner, and a little worn, the skin translucent as though she would soon fade away altogether.

"Alberic," she muttered, and he had to bend close to hear her words. "You came to me."

Two hours later Canon Alberic quitted the chamber and its still and silent occupant in the bed. He expressed no surprise to find Henri leaning against the tapestry-covered wall outside. In truth he was too exhausted and too low in spirits to care what his brother had overheard. He looked at Henri with dead eyes, the eyes of a man who has gazed into the pit until his soul has been consumed. He would have passed him without a word, but Henri seized him by the arm.

"Very touching," he sneered, pressing his face close to the Canon's. "She loved you all this time, and not me."

Canon Alberic shook off the restraining hand. "She is dead," he said shortly. "What can it matter now?"

"She was *my* wife."

"She told me about her life with you," said the Canon and the look he gave his brother was so scorching that anyone with a shred of conscience would have withered under it; Henri de Mauléon was unabashed, however.

"What of it? She was my property, Alberic. You may think you had her heart but I possessed her person. Remember that. For twelve years, night and day, I owned her. Especially the night."

Henri spoke with such repulsive meaning that at last the Canon's temper boiled over.

"May God damn you to hell, Henri."

Only his habitual awareness of the self-discipline required of a clergyman prevented him from knocking his brother down. He thrust his way past Henri de Mauléon and strode away without once looking back, even when his brother's mocking laughter sounded in his ears. When he regained the ground floor he ordered his horse to be saddled and brought around, heedless of the falling snow and the oncoming night.

The journey home was a lonely and terrible one, as the icy cold cut into him and an even deeper agony bit into his soul. He hunched over the horse's neck, his hands in their heavy gloves frozen into claws and his eyes narrowed to slits against the chill wind. Yet he never doubted that he would reach home safely. One searing idea carried him onwards through the whirling flakes, making him grind his teeth as he rode. *Henri shall pay. He shall pay.*

It was remarked amongst the other clergy of the chapter that Canon Alberic was much changed by his night's excursion in the snow. The Canon was a well-respected person, but up until that time it had generally been the accepted view that his bent lay more towards practical duties than abstract theology. Now, however, the focus of Canon Alberic's interest made such a *volte face* that it could not fail to be noticed even by the more dull-witted of his peers. It was supposed that he had had some species of revelation as he rode through the frozen darkness, perhaps some *memento mori* or actual vision of the hereafter. At any rate he now exhibited a hitherto unknown preoccupation with divine retribution and to what extent it might be accomplished though the agency of human hands. Further evidence of his deepening piety was seen in his frequent questioning of the older members of the chapter clergy about the history of the cathedral of Sainte-Marie, and particularly about the former bishop Bertrand de Got, later Pope Clement V, who so extended and embellished it. The bishop was said to have confiscated from the persecuted Knights Templar the seal ring of Solomon, by which he directed the demons of the air and the earth and under the earth, and to have concealed this ring in the cathedral at Comminges, to prevent the uninitiated from using it. It would be a great thing for the chapter, said the Canon, if the seal could be found, but in spite of all his energy his investigations appeared to come to nothing.

On the night of December 12th, 1694, when the last candles had been extinguished and the town of St. Bertrand de Comminges slumbered under the stars, the silence at the heart of the old cathedral was broken by the sound of footsteps moving lightly and stealthily across the tiled floor. A drawn-out creak and a dim rectangle appeared in the inky blackness as the south door was opened.

Canon Alberic de Mauléon, wrapped in a cloak to stave off the bitter cold, stepped out into the cloister. Under his arm he carried a long staff made of ash wood and in his hands he clasped a rectangular package, which the silvery moonlight glancing through the arches of the colonnade revealed as a leather-bound book. A rapid pulse in his throat belied the rigid set of his features. Hard by the cathedral's south wall he stopped, and placed the volume upon the flat top of one of the tombs that stood there, handling it gingerly as though he disdained to touch it. He stood for a few moments, with his hand pressed to his breast as though his heart pained him. His lips moved almost imperceptibly.

"Some spirits there be that are created for vengeance, and in their fury lay on sore strokes."

With that, he regained his courage. From within the cloak he produced various small objects which he ranged upon the tomb by the book, amongst them a fat yellow altar candle. Using a tinder box he lit the candle, and by its light he made his preparations with hands that trembled only slightly.

An observer, had he cared to stand behind the south door of the cathedral in the dark at that time of night, might have seen the sudden bloom of a second light, one which burned with a flickering, bluish glare. But no-one lurked there to see the Canon step backwards with an oath, and then hold his ground, though he put up a hand to shield his eyes. The other hand held the open book. The hand shook but his grip upon the volume did not falter.

There ensued a conversation of which only the Canon's side could have been clearly heard.

"*Quid tibi nomen?*"

The reply was uttered in a droning sibilant voice, like the howling of the night wind across the bleakness of a desert.

"*Ornias,*" repeated the Canon in a voice rimed with dread. He gathered himself with an effort. "*Inveniamne?*"

Again the terrible voice spoke.

The Canon strained to listen. "*Ubi est?*"

When the response came, a flicker of triumph crossed the Canon's face, in spite of the high tension. Three more questions, and he was done.

"*Te dimitto in nomine patris, et filiis, et spiritus sancti.*"

With a shriek like the rending of metal the demon vanished. In the sudden darkness Canon Alberic sagged against one of the carved inner columns of the cloister, almost swooning with the release of pent-up terror. It was some time before he was sufficiently master of himself to clear away the traces of his night's work.

A day or two later, the Canon was observed to wear a very fine old ring with a distinctive design upon it, which might have been taken to be a star or hexagram. A number of the members of the chapter having commented upon it, however, the Canon appeared to have decided that it was an unfitting ornament for a man of the cloth; at any rate it was seen no more upon his finger.

For several evenings Canon Alberic worked alone late into the night. The stream of his intellectual energy appeared to have reverted to its old course, for he spent the evenings working upon a drawing in sepia ink. It seemingly required great concentration, since he locked the door of his room against unforeseen interruptions. In spite of the taunting remarks of his brother Henri de Mauléon so many years previously, the work of inking designs upon a paper might not be conceived to be entirely incompatible with Christian duties; the early patristic writers cited a number of cases in which written designs or legends might be employed in the dismissal (or indeed the control) of the infernal beings. It may be assumed, however, that the result of Canon Alberic's labours was unsatisfactory, whether artistically or otherwise, since upon enquiry by a brother canon he reported that he had destroyed it.

On the feast of Saint Chaeromon, Canon Alberic once again sought permission to ride to the estate of his brother Henri. There was, he said, a long-standing discord between himself and his brother that was entirely unfitting for a Christian clergyman, and he wished to make his peace with Henri de Mauléon before the celebration of the birth of Him who came to end all conflicts. The application having been readily granted, Canon Alberic made haste to the Château de Mauléon.

His brother received him in the salon, where the fire was banked up and an extravagant number of candles were burning against the winter gloom. He did not bother to stand up when the Canon entered the room, nor did he offer his visitor a glass of the fine old cognac that sat within easy reach.

"So, brother Alberic, have you come to see whether I have gone to the devil or not?" was his fraternal greeting.

The Canon made him a bow. "On the contrary, Henri. I have come to make peace."

"Peace? What for?" Henri laughed cynically, wiping his mouth. "Come, come, brother Alberic. You did not ride for an hour in these temperatures to make some milksop declaration of regret. What is it you want? Out with it. A golden *Louis* for some benevolent project?" His lip curled in a sneer. "Or is it for yourself? You finally tired of the love of God and now you want to buy yourself a woman?"

Canon Alberic kept his temper with an effort. "Indeed I do not, Henri," he said evenly. "I seek nothing but your forgiveness for my rash words when we last met; indeed I have brought you a gift."

Henri de Mauléon grunted. "A gift? Well, let me see it then." His expression of bored cynicism rapidly turned to one of disgust. "What's this? Some canting book of prayers? It has a very pretty binding, Alberic, but you might have saved yourself the expense." He cast the book aside.

"It is a collection of very valuable manuscripts," said Canon Alberic. "Rare and costly, more suited to a gentleman's library than that of a humble canon."

"Well, there it may rest," returned his brother. "I'm obliged to you, Alberic, but you know better than to think I would read such a thing."

"Indeed I do," said Canon Alberic in a very low voice. "But I am content that it is in your possession."

"Fool," retorted Henri. He reached for the cognac. "You begin to bore me very much, Alberic. You may leave."

Once more the Canon bowed. "*Adieu*, Henri." A moment later he had gone.

On the night of the Feast of Saint Sylvester, 1701, when the ground sparkled with frost and few ventured out into the frigid darkness, the narrow streets of Saint Bertrand de Comminges rang once more to the sound of iron-shod hooves. A single horseman, well-muffled against the cold, rode up the hill to the heart of the town. He drooped in the saddle as though exhausted, and when he reached the cathedral square and dismounted, he almost fell to the ground. A stray servant of the church, hurrying home for his *dîner*, saw that the man was well-dressed, went to his assistance and to his urgent enquiry gave directions to the house where Canon Alberic lived.

Thus it was that at a quarter to ten the Canon was roused from his nightly devotions by a fusillade of knocking at the outer door.

"Alberic, Alberic!" cried a voice that was as familiar to him as his own, although it was hoarse with some terrible passion.

"He will waken the whole chapter," said the Canon grimly to himself, and hastened to unbar the door. Upon the instant the caller fell into his arms, and for several seconds their faces were only inches apart.

"Henri," gasped the Canon. Indeed he was shocked at the sight of Henri de Mauléon. The last time he had seen his brother, Henri had borne all the marks of a luxurious and self-indulgent life: the all too-solid covering of flesh, the florid complexion of the toper. Now, five years later, he was thinner than Alberic himself, as starved-looking as any religious ascetic, and his features, once richly tinted, were so pale that they appeared almost grey. The blue hollows in his cheeks gave him the appearance of a man in the extremity of mortal illness.

"Alberic—brother—for the love of God, you must help me."

Henri de Mauléon clung to Canon Alberic as a drowning man grasps at a floating spar, and yet the Canon

seemed disinclined to prolong the contact. He helped
Henri to a chair and then stepped back, glancing about
as he did so with an anxious air. Was it his imagination,
or had the air darkened in the room? He watched Henri
settle back in the chair, his head falling back to reveal the
sickly pallor of his throat, and then he hurried to fetch a
glass of wine, which he handed over at arm's length. After
that he went outdoors to see to Henri's horse, which was
stamping restlessly in the chill air.

He returned inside and stood with his back to the
stone wall, looking at his brother.

"Henri, you cannot stay here."

His brother drained the glass. "Alberic, you must help
me. He is with me almost constantly now—I sense his
approach—"

"Who is with you?" snapped the Canon in a state of
irritable nervousness. "You arrived alone, Henri."

"Not alone," croaked his brother. "Never alone. Night
and day, five years . . . Alberic, I have sinned, but it is a
sore punishment." He stretched out a palsied hand, which
Canon Alberic forebore to touch. "You must help me."

"You must pray to God for forgiveness," said the
Canon, but his cheeks were pale and his voice trembled.

"I have prayed to Him a thousand times," said Henri
hoarsely. "He is deaf to me."

"God is deaf to no-one who truly repents—"

"*You* must help me," cried Henri de Mauléon. "Alberic!
Alberic!" A shudder ran through his body and the eyes
rolled in his head. "He is coming!" he shrieked, twisting
in terror in his seat.

"Henri," cried the Canon in a high savage voice that
shocked the other into momentary silence. "I shall go to
the cathedral and fetch a censer and holy water and bless
you that this affliction may leave you."

"Don't leave me!" screamed his brother, struggling to rise, but he was too weak. As he fell back into his chair in an agony of despair, Canon Alberic quitted the house and closed the door behind him with a resounding bang.

For a moment Canon Alberic stood with his back against the door, looking over the rooftops to the black bulk of the cathedral of Sainte-Marie outlined against the night sky. In those few seconds, a mighty struggle raged within his breast. At last he turned and tried the door, but it was already immoveable. Instead he turned again and strode rapidly up to the cathedral square. He knelt on the freezing stones before the west door and bent his head in an attitude of supplication, and there he remained for a long time, neither moving nor speaking; not praying, but reflecting what he should do.

At length, stiff, weary and chilled to the bone, he arose and walked slowly home.

This time the door opened easily at his touch. The stone chamber within was silent, and deadly cold. The fire that had blazed so merrily in the grate had burnt down completely, leaving nothing but blackened ashes. Already the insides of the window panes sparkled with frost. In the armchair Henri de Mauléon lay dead, with great scratches down his cheeks where he had thrust his own fingernails into the flesh. His mouth gaped open in a silent scream, so wide that it must well-nigh have cracked the cartilage in his jaws, and the whites of his eyes showed where they had rolled back into his head. The bluish hands in his lap were bloody, the fingernails black with it.

Canon Alberic pressed a hand to his mouth as he stood by the entrance and gazed upon his brother's body.

"Oh God," he said to himself. "Five years." But then he thought, "*She* suffered for twelve." He closed the door and went to work.

The Canon was a lean man but he was hardened by years of labour and self-denial, and besides, Henri de Mauléon was no longer as corpulent as he had been five years ago. It was relatively easy to move the body to the Canon's bedroom and strip it. Henri was pitifully thin, worn down by his trials. The Canon's night-shirt fitted him perfectly.

Alberic removed the wig from his brother's head with care. Underneath it the hair was cropped, but clearly Henri had neglected it just as he had neglected his other bodily attributes. It had grown sufficiently that with a little judicious trimming it resembled the Canon's own sober style well enough.

Stepping into Henri de Mauléon's clothes was a curious experience; Alberic was unused to the luxury of such costly and fashionable things, having worn the dress of a canon for so long. It was distasteful to him to don his brother's wig, but necessary all the same.

All the time he was conscious of a growing feeling of being watched by an unseen presence. His hands trembled as he fastened Henri's greatcoat about him. *Of course*, he thought to himself. *I am Henri's heir, since he has no child. All that belonged to him now belongs to me, and that includes—the book.* He began to think that he must ride for the Château de Mauléon as soon as possible, and do what he could to dismiss his unwanted companion.

It took five years to wear Henri down, he reminded himself, but still his nerves were so affected by the events of the evening that he dreaded to bear too long the sense of being followed, much less to see his pursuer. The mere idea of it made the hair stand up on the back of his neck.

In his haste to be gone from the house, he very nearly missed the object that lay on the floor at the side of the chair in which Henri had died. Had he not turned sharply for one last glance about the room, he would have left it behind him. It was a leather hunting pouch.

When he picked it up, he was immediately conscious of its weight. There was something in it. Even before he had undone the buckle and peered inside, he knew what it was. *The book. Henri brought the damned book with him.*

He resisted the temptation to hurl the volume away from him. Instead he closed up the bag again with trembling fingers.

Why did he bring the book with him? Did he know?

He reminded himself how improbable this was. The paper he had inserted into the book was concealed between two leaves at the very back. Even supposing Henri had read that far, it was unlikely he would have found it. More likely the poor wretch had carried the volume with him because of the holy texts within, reasoning that it would offer him some protection from the infernal thing that pursued him. Very possibly it was the nearest thing to a Bible Henri had owned.

What shall I do with it? For a moment Alberic was tempted to build up the fire again and cast the book into it, priceless manuscripts and all. And yet as he stood there irresolutely, with the darkness seeming to beat about his head like great wings, there came to him an idea, a far better idea.

It would require but one uncomfortable night, and that was half over already. He took up a candle and carried the bag with the book in it to the desk where he habitually wrote his letters and other documents. Steeling himself, he laid the hunting pouch on the desk and drew out the book. A little judicious work with his pocket-knife and the hidden paper was removed from its hiding-place.

Alberic took out a ledger from his desk and cut out a fresh leaf with his knife. Upon this he proceeded to draw out a plan of the cathedral of Sainte-Marie, working swiftly from memory. There was no need to conceal his handwriting; it should be recognisable as his own—at least, recognisable as that of Canon Alberic de Mauléon, whose lifeless remains apparently occupied the bed upstairs. It was not difficult to embellish the plan with a number of esoteric-looking symbols and figures—he was, after all, a man with no little natural artistic talent.

After some thought he added some text to the plan, and also to the reverse of the drawing he had removed from the book. The wording was concise, but to the perceptive reader it told its story of hubristic impiety and savage nemesis with stark clarity. When he had completed his task and the ink had dried, he fixed the two leaves at the back of the volume, and placed the book itself in plain view in the centre of the desk, so that it might easily be found.

What to do with the remaining hours of darkness? He considered riding back to the château, but it occurred to him that Henri's presence in the town was unlikely to have passed unnoticed; he must have at least asked directions to the house. Rather than leave and return again the following day for the book, the less suspicious course of action was to spend the rest of the night under the Canon's roof. He might claim, indeed, that the Canon had sent for his brother Henri because he had foreseen the divine retribution that had clearly overtaken him, and had feared to be alone. How glad he was now that self-discipline had prevented him from complaining of Henri's offences to his fellow canons! There was little reason for any of them to suspect a feud.

He remained in the house, therefore, but he kept a vigil downstairs, and he sat with his back to the wall.

Morning came at last, staining the winter sky a dirty grey and then a lurid off-white colour that presaged the coming of snow. As daylight illuminated the chamber where Alberic sat straight-backed against the stone wall, the apprehension that had gripped him began to fade a little. He arose and went to a press in the corner of the room, from which he took some blankets and laid them over the chair nearest the remains of the fire to give the impression that he had slept there. When a servant girl appeared some time later to sweep the hearth and prepare Canon Alberic's lunch, she was taken aback to find a fine gentleman—"the very image of the Canon himself, only handsomer"—seated at the Canon's table, having made himself a breakfast of bread and cheese from the Canon's cupboard.

The gentleman, who was discovered to be Henri de Mauléon, observed to the girl that he thought the Canon rose rather late; he had supposed that his brother would have attended Matins, but he had seen nothing of him that morning. Eventually she was persuaded to accompany him upstairs to ascertain that the Canon had not been taken ill in the night.

Shortly afterwards, the street rang to a series of loud shrieks. The servant girl had had hysterics at the sight of the body; but Henri de Mauléon remained wonderfully calm, although he looked exceedingly pale.

In due course the book was examined, the Canon's brother having declared that it held some malevolent significance for the dead man. The two leaves at the back were discovered, the other canons decided that they were out of their depth, and the Bishop himself was informed.

The Bishop took one look at the plan of the cathedral with its arcane symbols, and the ugly drawing that accompanied it, and proposed to confiscate the book on the spot. That such a thing should exist was very bad;

that one of his own canons should have created it was appalling. There was nothing to do but suppress it at once.

"I had intended to take it away and destroy it myself," said Henri de Mauléon in a mild tone that would have surprised his friends or indeed his servants, had they heard it. "It appears to be my brother's property." And he touched the arms of Mauléon stamped upon the cover.

The Bishop's already florid face flushed brick red. He might have spoken hastily, but the fine attire of the Canon's brother gave him pause; clearly he was a personage not to be toyed with. It occurred to him that Henri de Mauléon could cause a considerable amount of annoyance to the chapter and to himself, should he wish. He replied respectfully that he understood, but that if *Monseigneur* wished to rid himself of a volume so clearly dangerous and inconsistent with the virtue and honour of his house, the chapter library would gladly accept it as a donation, and there it might remain in seclusion, safely under lock and key.

To argue would have created more suspicion.

"You accept it as a gift to the chapter?" asked Henri de Mauléon formally.

"Willingly," said the Bishop.

And thus the book passed into the possession of the cathedral itself, along with a certain old-fashioned ring that Henri said had belonged to his brother. There it must have remained, and the Bishop must have kept his promise to secure it from all eyes, as it was the only volume to escape the revolutionary *auto-da-fé* a century later, in which all the Episcopal papers were consumed.

As for Henri de Mauléon, he returned to his château a changed man. The death of his brother the Canon had touched him very deeply; from that day forward he spurned his drinking companions, cared for the tenants on his estate with energy and kindness, and never failed to keep the Sabbath. In time he grew to be esteemed and even envied, not just for his wealth but for the great affection all those about him bore for him. He never married again, but he kept green the memory of his wife Isabelle, and when he died in bed at the ripe old age of eighty-three he was laid to rest beside her.

The Calvary at Banská Bystrica

"You knew my brother, of course," said my friend, looking at me over the top of his half-moon spectacles.

"*Knew*?" I said. "Past tense? Does this mean you've heard something?"

"Good heavens, no," he replied a little brusquely. "Do you think I would still be living like this if I had?" He wriggled the stockinged feet which he had extended towards the little gas fire. A toe protruded through a hole in one sock; he regarded it almost meditatively, thinking perhaps of the large portion which would be his were his only brother discovered to be dead, instead of just missing. Some might have thought his remark singularly callous and lacking in brotherly sentiment; however I knew how things had lain between them, and furthermore I had met Robert Montague and had disliked him immensely.

The pair of us sat in companionable silence for a little while, gazing at the blue gas flames. I poured myself another glass of claret; it was not a bad one—I had brought it with me, since I knew my friend never ran to such things. Eventually he said, without looking at me, "You know, I don't think he *will* turn up, ever."

"Oh?" I said, and waited, gazing into the claret's blood-red depths.

"No," he said in a decided tone, as though trying to argue someone down. He fell silent again for a moment, then looked at me sideways and said, "I went out there, you know. I did try to find him."

"Out where?" I asked. It was news to me that there was even a known location at which Robert Montague might have met with an accident, been knifed by pickpockets or succumbed to an early heart attack. As far as I knew, he had just stopped communicating with anyone, whether his brother, his lawyer or the agent who procured the publication of his obscenely pretentious books about Art. He had been travelling around the Continent, either on a sabbatical or perhaps collecting material for his next assault upon the Art world, and had suddenly ceased all contact with everyone. Up until then he had been a regular communicator; indeed an ego like his could barely tolerate the social vacuum of independent travel. Still, this might not necessarily mean anything sinister had occurred; he might have taken it into his head that he needed absolute isolation to work on the material he had gathered; he might have moved on to a place where the postal service was bad or non-existent, and technical development at too primitive a stage to allow for electronic mail; heaven knows!—he might have broken his wrist and been unable to write or even type. However, the news that there even was an "out there" did cast a rather negative light upon the matter.

"Slovakia," said my friend, rubbing his hands together. He glanced at me. "The Low Tatras, to be precise."

"The Low Tatras?" I repeated, rolling the words around my tongue as though tasting an unknown vintage. "Isn't that a mountain range? And aren't there some High Tatras as well?"

He looked at me again a little quizzically, as if ascertaining whether I was being facetious.

"Go on," I said hastily.

"I last heard from him in the spring," said my friend. "He wrote to me several times from Banská Bystrica. Some letters and a card."

I raised my eyebrows. Robert Montague and his brother had hardly been in the state of close fraternal relations that would merit the frequent exchange of letters.

"I know," said my friend wryly. "We weren't much in the habit of writing. But the thing is: Robert had decided to marry." He glanced back at the fire again, musing. "I suppose he thought blood was thicker than water and he wanted to share his news with me, since I was the only family he had. I still have the letters; I took them with me when I went out there, and I can't imagine throwing them out. He sent some sketches too. I'll fish them out in a minute. Anyway, the first letter arrived after he had been at Banská Bystrica about a fortnight. I'm not sure what drew him to that particular town in the first place; in fact he was downright disparaging about it—said the town museum was full of the most stupid things and most of the interesting churches were locked. You know how Robert was. I can't think how he came to stay in the town for longer than a day or two, unless he intended to use it as a base to visit other places in the area. But that, of course, was before he met this girl. Her name was Lubica and she had some sort of job relating to tourism in the town; she worked on the front desk at one of the museums I think—or at least he met her in the museum; I'm not really clear about that. Anyway it seems to have been a whirlwind romance because the next thing you know he's proposed to the girl and she's said yes." My friend paused. "I've got a sketch of her somewhere here which Robert enclosed in the first of his letters." He fished around amongst the untidy heap of papers on the little table at his elbow. "Look."

I took the dog-eared piece of paper from him and inspected the little sketch. It was well-done; Robert Montague may not have been able to write a straightforward phrase to save his life, but he drew beautifully. There was a quality about the drawing which transcended anything a photograph could have achieved; the faint smile which played around Lubica's lips was strongly suggestive of personality, and the gaze of those large limpid eyes was far more engagingly expressed than in a photographic print, when red-eye and that awful flash-bleached look so often divest the subject of any intelligible expression.

"She can't be more than about twenty-five," I remarked. "And very pretty." An image of Robert Montague's florid and pompous visage came to mind. Beauty and the Beast just wasn't in it. What on earth could this beautiful young woman have found to admire in Robert Montague?

"Half Robert's age, yes," said my friend. He stretched out his hand to take back the sketch. Tucking it face-down back into the pile of papers, he went on: "And I'm sure you're wondering what she saw in him. Well, I wonder about it too, but Robert didn't. Here—" he continued, passing me another paper, "You can read what he said for himself."

I perused the letter with distaste. I am not the sort of person who can comfortably read other people's correspondence, though I supposed in these circumstances it might be acceptable, if only to shed some light upon the mystery of what had become of Robert Montague. And then it was such a repellent letter in itself—full of the author's overblown ego and compulsive posturing. I remember he referred to somewhere that he and the girl intended to visit, making pretentious comparisons with the Kelîsâ-yé Vânk in Esfahân. But worst of all was his attitude towards the girl herself. It was manifestly clear that Robert Montague considered that he was doing her an enormous favour by entering into an engagement with her; underlying his every remark was the assumption that a girl from the rural depths of Eastern Europe would give her right arm to "catch" a sophisticated foreigner from the affluent West. He made patronising little comments about Lubica's habits and opinions, implying throughout that she would be much improved when he had remade her in his own image. He made jovial asides about the unsophisticated lifestyle of her family, and outlined repulsive little plans for patronising them once he had joined his splendid lineage to their modest one. If I had disliked Robert Montague before, my opinion was confirmed ten times over when I read that letter, and more than ever I wondered at Lubica's agreeing to have him. I handed the letter back to my friend, holding it ironically by one corner.

"His last letter was sent from Banská Bystrica at the end of April," he continued. "And after that—nothing. Not a word to me nor to anyone else—not even Rufus." Rufus was Robert Montague's agent, as noxious a personality as Robert himself; the two of them were naturally as thick as thieves.

"I wasn't particularly concerned at first," went on my friend. "When I didn't hear anything more, I assumed that Robert's sudden outburst of fraternal affection had worn off, and he was amusing himself with patronising his new fiancée instead. But eventually Rufus got in touch— it seems he was expecting to hear from Robert about some ghastly tome they were planning to launch upon the unsuspecting public, and Robert had overrun some deadline by ten days. Rufus was pretty annoyed about it, and since he couldn't get hold of Robert he took it out on me instead. Of course, I couldn't care less about the deadline, but I did start to wonder whether everything was quite as it should be. When Rufus rang back a week later and said Robert *still* hadn't got in touch, we started to discuss what we should do about it. Rufus was all for calling the police, but I said I didn't see what good this would do. I didn't suppose Interpol were going to go rushing off to Banská Bystrica to investigate a middle-aged writer who hadn't contacted his agent for a couple of weeks. And in fact when I did eventually try to contact someone in authority, this was more or less what they said; Robert was a grown man and just because he had chosen not to write was not a cause for investigation, unless we had any other more concrete reason for suspecting foul play, which of course we hadn't. Well, spring wore into summer and we still hadn't heard a thing, so I started to think that I would have to do something about it myself. I must admit I was puzzled. If something had happened to Robert, a heart attack or something, surely this Lubica would have tried to contact his family? Unless Lubica herself were involved, that is: but even then it didn't make much sense. If she were a con-woman or a gold digger, why kill the goose that lays the golden eggs? The more I thought about it, the odder it seemed. And eventually I decided to go to Banská Bystrica myself and see if I could find him. I am a man of limited means"—and here my friend gave me a dry smile—"but I bought myself a ticket on one of the budget airlines, and once I got to Slovakia of course everything was amazingly cheap. I thought I could manage a week or at a pinch ten days, and I hoped by that time I would have found Robert, or at least discovered where he had gone next. Quite possibly I would find him in the arms of the lovely Lubica, and not at all delighted to have a visitor from home to interrupt his romantic interlude, but at least then I could tell him to contact

Rufus before the man had a coronary about the missed deadline, and I could meet the woman who was deluded enough to contemplate becoming my sister-in-law.

"Well, I arrived in Banská Bystrica and established myself in a little hotel near the centre. It's an odd mixture of a town; on the one hand there is the wide square lined with baroque buildings in a patchwork of fading colours, the foaming fountains and the clock tower which plays a charming little melody instead of chiming; on the other hand the awful clusters of Soviet-style blocks which congest the modern sections of the town, drearily dilapidated and scarred with graffiti. I wondered in which part of the town Lubica and her family had their home. Once I had got my bearings, it didn't take me long to find the little pension from which Robert had sent his last letter. The landlady didn't speak much English and no German at all but I think she must have realised who I was from the family resemblance and then she became very voluble, chattering on in Slovakian and waving her hands around, oblivious or uncaring of the fact that I understood not one word. Eventually she led me upstairs and showed me into a little room overlooking the street. There was a bed and a sink and a little wooden table and chair, these last placed next to the window, so that the sunlight spilled across the tabletop. On the table was a heap of things which I soon identified as Robert's; mainly papers covered in Robert's bold handwriting. On the chair was a portmanteau which appeared to have been rather hastily packed; I thought perhaps the landlady herself had thrust all Robert's belongings into it, intending to store it or even throw it out if her lodger failed to return. I looked around the room a little, opening cupboard doors and drawers, but there was nothing else of Robert's to be seen, so in the end I started to pack it all up to take with me. Before I left I offered the landlady some money from my fast-diminishing store, thinking that Robert had perhaps left an unpaid bill. She took what seemed a very modest amount out of it and handed the rest back to me. I hesitated for a moment, standing on her doorstep with my brother's belongings in my arms, but it seemed the limited communication between us was at an end. She said: '*Dakujem*,' and then quietly closed the door, leaving me in the street.

"Anyhow, after a moment's consideration I went to a little café on the main square, ordered myself a coffee and settled down to go through Robert's things. The portmanteau revealed little of interest, although I was surprised to find Robert's glasses case at the bottom. The glasses were not inside it. It seemed odd to think that he would take them with him but not the case. The other things were mainly items of clothing. There was also a shaving brush and a travel alarm clock whose battery had gone flat; the hands of the clock were frozen at twenty-two minutes past five. I piled the things back into the portmanteau and started sorting through the papers instead. Most of them were notes for a new book about Eastern European Art which Robert was evidently planning. After reading a couple of pages I gave up in disgust; whatever else may have come of Robert's trip to Slovakia the demise of that book can only be seen in a positive light. As well as the notes there was a little spiral-bound notebook. At first I thought it was completely unused, but on the second page I found an address written in an unknown hand. The handwriting was fairly poor and wholly unlike Robert's, which though flourishing was extremely clear. The name at the top was *Lubica*, though I could make little of the surname apart from the initial M. Then there was what seemed to be a street name ending in what could have been 123 or 125, and after that a completely unintelligible scrawl which might have been a postcode but could equally have been the name of a district, and which terminated in one single legible word, *Tajov*. This was progress indeed; if I could only work out what the rest of the address was, I could start with a visit to Lubica herself.

"There was one last item of interest amongst the papers, and that was a single snapshot of Robert himself. Monstrously inflated though Robert's ego was, I was still a little surprised that he had kept this photograph of himself. Although the picture was technically good, that is to say, it was neither sun-bleached nor loweringly dark, and it was perfectly sharp, the composition left a bit to be desired. First of all Robert himself was standing in an awkward posture slightly to the left of centre, leaning in slightly and with his left arm held at an angle away from his body. It was a stiff and unnatural-looking pose. And then whoever had taken the photograph had included half of something at the side, far over to the left, so that the whole effect was rather lopsided. The thing at the left looked like a little building, although when I looked a little more closely I decided it must be something different; the scale was much too small for it to be a proper building of any sort as it only came up to the height of my brother's head. It might have been a dovecot or even something as prosaic as a bus shelter. It was painted white all over, and I could just see a section of black frame, which might perhaps be the edge of a window. There was not much else to be seen in the photograph, the remaining area being taken up with foliage. I wondered whether Lubica had taken the picture; certainly it would have been considerably more interesting if she had been in it, alongside my brother. I stared at Robert's well-fed features for a moment, then put the photograph down with a sigh. It would be so very much easier to investigate if I spoke even rudimentary Slovakian, or knew someone who did.

"Well, on this occasion it seems my prayers were answered. After leaving the café I began to wander downhill along the main street, with no particular aim but perhaps to come across a tourist information office or some such place where I might try to make myself understood sufficiently well to ask about the address I had found. It was not long before I passed a small arcade between the shops, and saw a little blackboard standing outside, the word *Sommelier* inscribed on it in large white letters. In the corner of the blackboard someone had stuck a little union flag to indicate that English was spoken here. I went into the arcade and discovered a tiny shop with three walls covered with shelves of Slovakian wines and the space by the front window occupied by a desk at which sat a young man working at a laptop. He arose as I came in, giving one of the keys a flourishing tap to show that I now had his full attention.

" '*Rozprávate po anglicky?*' I attempted in my best phrase-book Slovakian.

" 'Of course,' he replied in perfect English. 'How may I help you?'

"His name was Jano, and a more perfect aide to my investigations I could not have found. Not only did he speak beautifully correct English, but he was wildly keen to practise speaking it with me. I had foreseen that I should have to buy several bottles of Slovakian wine—an unwanted expense—to pay for his assistance in deciphering Lubica's address, but this turned out to be quite unnecessary. In fact he pressed a complimentary glass on me whilst we pored over Robert's notebook. He squinted at the handwriting for some time, a slight frown creasing his brow. Once it seemed as though he were about to say something, but he changed his mind and continued to stare at the scrawl on the page. At last he said: 'This address is not in Banská Bystrica, you know.'

"No?" I said, disappointed.

" 'No, it is in Tajov, a very small village,' he told me, tapping the page with one forefinger.

" 'Is it far?' I asked, my heart sinking.

" 'Not far,' said Jano decisively. 'I can drive you if you like.'

"Of course, I did like, and I was profuse in my thanks to my new friend. I arranged to meet him later in the afternoon. Just as I was about to go, I remembered something. Fishing amongst Robert's papers, I dug out the photograph of Robert and held it out to Jano.

" 'I don't suppose you recognise this place, do you?'

"He looked at it, and I could see at once that he did. A curious expression came over his face, like a shadow flitting across it. Then his jaw tightened a little and it was impossible to tell whether he was somehow impressed or merely bored.

" 'I think that is the Calvary hill in Tajov,' he said slowly.

" 'Oh,' I said, then: 'My brother must have visited it. Maybe I could take a look whilst we are in the village?'

" 'Yes, maybe,' he said, with a very slight inflection on the second word. Then he shrugged, smiled and me and said, 'Okay.' It was a polite dismissal. I thanked him and went back outside into the sunshine, to wander around the town until the arranged time. I went back to the hotel and dropped off the portmanteau and most of the papers, but kept the notebook and the photograph with me. Then I sauntered about admiring the tall faded buildings with their ornate façades, and watching the people who bustled to and fro. There were relatively few foreign visitors apart from myself, and most of them seemed to be Germans. I went into a little museum on the main square and looked at a collection of antique clocks, strange old rifles and shakoes. I wondered whether Robert had been here, whether this was perhaps even the museum in which he had met Lubica. But the person on the front desk was a woman of about fifty-five who spoke no English, only a little German, and there was no sign of any other staff. At length I heard the pleasant sound of the clock tower chiming out its melody at the top of the square, and I left the museum and went off to find Jano.

"Tajov proved to be very close to Banská Bystrica indeed: it was really a satellite of the main town. It was about twenty minutes past four when we arrived in the village, and the sunshine was still fierce. Jano parked the car in a square of tarmac outside the post office, which was closed, with all the blinds drawn down and the front door locked. We got out and stood there irresolutely in the hot sun.

" 'Do you know where this is?' I asked Jano, holding up the notebook with the cover folded back to show the address.

"He shook his head. 'I will have to ask.' His tone was flat and unenthusiastic. I was puzzled and slightly irritated, to be truthful: he had been falling over himself to help when I first approached him, and now he seemed apathetic and reluctant. But I decided that I would have to press on with it, even if it meant forcing the issue: there was not likely to be any better chance to investigate than there was now, when I was here in Tajov with a native-speaking Slovakian and a car.

" 'What about in there?' I asked, pointing at a sign reading *Víno* hanging outside what looked like a series of lock-up garages. So we crossed the road and started the first of our enquiries. After the wine shop we tried the grocery store, and after that we tried the little local bar with the familiar *Corgon* sign hanging over the door. Then we tried asking anyone we could find who was in his or her front garden. With a little prodding Jano even knocked on a couple of doors, but the story was the same everywhere. No-one had heard of Lubica, or so it seemed; they seemed somehow offended by the enquiry. And Jano said that he was no nearer working out where number 123 or 125 in the illegible street was to be found.

" 'Well.' I said it almost as a reproach. I sighed heavily, reluctant to admit that we had reached a dead end. 'Look, Jano, maybe the address is wrong. But what about the picture? Didn't you say that was somewhere in Tajov? Could we try and find out where?'

"He studied me for a few moments, his expression unreadable. Then he said: 'You mean the Calvary hill? But your brother just visited it. Why should he be there now?'

" 'I don't—' I began, then took off my glasses and rubbed my eyes with the back of my hand. I was hot and thirsty and tired, and this was turning into a wild goose chase. But all the same, Robert *was* my brother, and irritating though he could be, I felt I owed it to him to pursue the matter as far as I could. I must admit that by this time I had pretty much given up all hope of finding him anywhere in Banská Bystrica or the surrounding area. I just wanted to tell myself I had done all I could, and then go home. I tried to tell Jano this, but the words were coming out all wrong in my frustration. In the end he put his hand on my arm and suggested we go for a cold beer in the little bar whilst we decided what to do next. He was kindly, Jano was, and I think he had my best interests at heart, though at the time I thought him quite uncooperative.

"Anyway, we went into the bar and ordered a beer each, and then Jano went and spoke to the landlord at some length, all in Slovakian of course. I heard him say '*Anglican*' a few times, and they both looked my way. Then Jano came back to the table and started to give me directions to the Calvary hill.

" 'Wait a minute,' I said. 'Aren't you coming with me?'

" 'It's easy, you won't get lost,' he said by way of reply, and started sketching out the route on the tabletop with one finger. 'You go up the wooden steps here, and then you have to go right. If you go left you will walk for a great many hours until you are in Kremnica,' he informed me.

" 'Are you sure you won't come with me?' I pleaded.

" 'I will wait for you here,' he said imperturbably. 'I will order you another beer for when you come down.'

"Well, I had imposed on his good nature enough already, so I had to accept the situation. I got up and left him sitting at the little table staring into his beer, then walked outside into the late afternoon sunshine.

"In spite of what Jano had said about the impossibility of getting lost, it took me some time to find the way to the Calvary hill. There was no proper path—you had to walk up over a patch of grass, which did not even have the marks of feet, whether human or rabbits.

"Perhaps I should explain a little about the Calvary hill, since it was the first time I had ever seen one. There are a number of them in Slovakia, and elsewhere too for all I know, and some of them are a lot grander than this one. There is a better-known one near Banská Stiavnica—you can see the church at the top from the main road which passes it, and very imposing it looks, too. What you have is a pathway up a hill, with a series of stations at intervals on the way up; the stations often look like little shrines with a glass front, and inside there is usually a religious figure or scene. At the top of the hill is a church or chapel. On feast days the local people make a procession up the hill. It was one of the stations of the Tajov Calvary hill which Jano had apparently recognised in the photograph of Robert.

"Well, after a little wandering about, and a false start which nearly found me in someone's back garden, I discovered the way up to the Calvary hill. Really, if I had not known it was there, I would never have found it; everything was so overgrown, and the chapel at the top is surrounded with trees so that nothing of it can be seen from the village. The stations themselves start somewhere in the village below; there are four on the hill itself. Although the hill itself is not so very high, it is steep, and in the absence of a proper path it was hard going. I wondered when the last feast day had been; there certainly was no sign of anyone at all having been up here recently, much less a procession. The grass was almost up to my knees, which not only impeded my progress, but also made me nervous of the blood-sucking ticks and other insects with which the area abounds. Certainly the warm air was thick with the thrumming of cicadas. I stumped uphill as best I could, dodging the overhanging branches of trees. Exertion made my breath ragged, and I paused for a moment, breathing hard. As I stood there a patch of white amongst the tangled foliage caught my eye and I realised I had reached one of the stations. Curious, I pulled aside a branch to take a closer look. It was quite empty. All the panes of glass in the front window were intact, but there was nothing at all in the niche inside, apart from a few dead insects, their bunched legs like scribbles against the whitewashed interior. It was disappointing; I wondered whether Robert might have given up at this point, seeing that whatever examples of votive art had adorned the stations had been removed. Still, having come this far I was determined to go on.

"The second station was soon reached; this time the niche contained only a small gilded bracket in the shape of a cherub's head, upon which some object or statue had evidently resided in the past. Some knock had taken a large chip out of the cherub's upper lip, so that now the full cupid's bow resembled a hare lip. The blind eyes stared out obliviously. I laid an exploratory finger on the glass; it was cool, one spot of coldness in the seething heat of the afternoon. Staring in I could see that a spider had begun to spin a web from the cherub's cheek to the corner of the niche. It was an ugly thought, the jointed legs of the spider moving over the childish contours of the face. I turned away and went on up the hill.

"If I had expected to see anything dramatic in either of the other two stations, I was doomed to disappointment. Both were empty, as the first had been. The very last was missing a single pane of glass from the bottom of the window; a little heap of broken shards lay in the grass underneath, and at first I wondered how it had come there, envisaging something bursting out from inside, before I realised more prosaically that someone must have brushed them all out for neatness' sake, and then left them there in the absence of any suitable receptacle.

"Standing by the last station, a hand pressed to my side where I could feel a painful stitch, I was able at last to see the little church at the top of the hill, shaded by the trees which had grown up tall around it. It was constructed in a simple style, a one-storey building with a stubby tower; the walls had been covered with a plain pale-coloured wash and there was a little double door of stained wood with glass panels set into it at the front. It was in all ways an unremarkable-looking edifice, and yet there was something about it which struck me in an unpleasant way. Standing there silent and closed under its canopy of trees, it made me think of someone who had lost their senses of sight and hearing, yet sat waiting, turning their head blindly from side to side, waiting for the touch that would tell them someone else was there. When I forced myself to start the final climb up to the little door I found myself walking carefully, so as to make as little sound as possible, lifting my feet above the long grasses which whispered against my trouser legs.

"The last few feet were almost a scramble, up a steep little bank clotted with moss. Then at last I stood at the step which led up to the church door. Even here in the shade of the tall trees the heat was oppressive. I could feel my shirt sticking to my back. Around me the air was still thick with the endless sawing sound of the hidden insects. I mounted the step and tried the door.

"Of course, it was locked. I tried the door once, then again, pressing a little harder on the handle in case it was merely stiff, but to no avail. Then I stepped up close to the glass panels and stared into the interior of the church. The arrangement inside was very plain; a central aisle with rows of wooden pews of crude construction ranged on either side. The ceiling was, I saw, quite low, and in the centre was a sort of ceiling rose through which there depended a thick crimson cord that I thought must be a bell-pull. At the very back of the church there was some sort of lectern, or perhaps there may even have been a proper pulpit, but I didn't notice these details very clearly because my attention was drawn to an enormous mural on the back wall. I am no expert on religious symbolism—Robert could have told you a lot more about it than I ever could—but it was pretty clearly a Last Judgement scene. There were several angels blowing the Last Trump on long horns, and on the left were a group whom I took to be the Righteous, in various attitudes of praise and being addressed by an angel. On the right side the resurrection of the Dead was depicted, with much weeping and wailing in dumb show. I found the depiction frankly distasteful; I remember there was a body curled like a great embryo within a shattered urn, and a grinning skeleton draped in some black garment, one arm thrown up with horrid energy. Presiding over all this was a patriarchal God with high-domed forehead and long flowing hair; at his left shoulder fluttered cherubs holding an open book upon which the letters *alpha* and *omega* were inscribed. It is impossible for me, with my imperfect knowledge of Art history, to say exactly when this painting might have been executed. My first thought was that it was rather crude, but upon further contemplation I had to admit that it had a certain vitality about it, and I began to see why Robert might have made his odious reference to the Kelîsâ-yé Vânk.

"As I stood there gazing through the glass, I was overwhelmed with a feeling of loss. I suddenly felt certain that I would never see Robert again. I knew now that I could go no further in my search. It had not been easy coming this far, and there was no further clue to be found. Jano, though friendly, was clearly unwilling to become any more involved, and without a forwarding address, without a reasonable level of spoken Slovakian, it was hopeless. I leaned my forehead against the glass and closed my eyes. It was like saying a prayer for the dead. In fact I think I did say something, something like, 'Where *are* you, Robert?' but in the lowest of miserable whispers, despairing of any reply.

"And then I heard a sound like a long-drawn-out breath, and I opened my eyes. I gazed once more into the dim interior of the church, and the next moment it was as if a streak of icy lightning ran its jagged path down my body. The church was *no longer empty*. There was someone—I thought it *was* a person—standing on the right-hand side at the other end of the church, close up to the mural and facing the wall, like a naughty child who has been made to stand in the corner. I say I *thought* it was a person, because although the torso and legs could clearly be seen, the head was sunk so low between the shoulders as to be invisible, and the arms also had been somehow pulled or folded in front of the body so that they could not be seen from behind. The body was absolutely naked, the flesh garishly white in the gloom and somehow flaccid. It reminded me of that disgusting painting by Goya, of Cronus devouring his children. And the worst of it was, I *recognised* the body. Low down on the flabby back there was a long, dark-brown mole, standing out like a splash of paint. I knew then. It was Robert.

"Perhaps I should have banged on the glass then, tried the door again, or even attempted to shoulder it down. But I didn't, and even now I am convinced it would not have worked. I was meant to *see*, but I could do nothing to change what happened.

"As I have said, the head and arms were invisible; now the torso itself began to undergo a curious change. Somehow—I can't describe it—it began to look hunched, although hunched is the wrong word because it implies muscular tension. There was no muscular action in that white flabby body, which looked as soft and boneless as dough. The two bulges at the shoulders, where the arms had been somehow drawn in front of the body, began to flatten out, and the dip where the head had fallen forward also began to smooth itself out so that the whole upper torso took on an unnatural tight rounded appearance. It looked as though the—as though Robert had tried to force his head and shoulders through a tight aperture, except that I knew there was only wall there, and the mural. And then I saw that the body was no longer standing with the feet flat on the floor of the church. In some way the knees had been drawn forwards like the head and arms, and upwards, so that the feet dangled above the floor, with the bare soles towards me. Like the rest of the body they were a dead unnatural white, and I noticed with a distant disgust that the toes were thickly rimed with black earth. The next instant and whatever force was pulling on the knees or legs gave another yank and the feet were pulled up tight under the sagging buttocks. I could not see who or what was exerting the force upon the body, but the effect was that of someone trying to haul a great sack full of some soft but heavy substance through a hole or orifice that was too small to admit it.

"All the time this loathsome process was going on, I could hear, or at least *sense*, sounds; perhaps I should say a *voice*. It was a sort of gasping; it might have been from exertion, or shock, or both, it was impossible to say, and it went on and on and on, like some obscene parody of childbirth, until I thought I should lose my wits if I listened for one second more. I squeezed my eyes tight shut, but then there came a compulsion so strong that I had to open them again, and I saw that the body had further folded up upon itself, so that the feet had now disappeared and all that was visible was the bulging mass of torso, clinging to the wall like some sort of insect's nest. The flesh no longer appeared flabby, such was the pressure of whatever force was being exerted upon it. Smaller and smaller and tighter and tighter it grew, until it looked like the cap of a great pallid mushroom, and then with horrible rapidity it shrank to nothing. At the same moment the maddening gasps ceased abruptly. I found myself staring at the mural, at the corpse like a foetus curled in the urn, and the death's head with its outflung arm. The painted surface appeared unbroken and undisturbed. I stood there with the cold perspiration trickling down my back and stared and stared at the wall, but nothing moved and there was absolutely no sound from anywhere. A moment later the insects started up again with their endless droning and the spell was broken. I started away from the glass and staggered back from the door.

"I need not describe the run back down to the village, with my legs almost buckling underneath me and my arms flailing wildly at the overhanging vegetation. Once I stumbled and almost ran into the side of one of those Calvary stations, and leapt back as though it had some contagion. It was a miracle I didn't break an ankle or worse. At last I reached the village and staggered on trembling legs into the little bar where Jano was waiting.

"When he saw me, Jano leapt to his feet with an exclamation, but although he was shocked I think he was not altogether surprised. He took me by the arm and led me to a chair. He offered me the beer he had promised, but I waved it away. I put my elbows on my knees and my head in my hands and clenched my hair between my fingers as though it would make the memory of that foul gasping go away. My whole body was shaking. At last Jano brought me a little glass of some spirit, I don't know what it was, and I swallowed the whole lot in one go. After that I felt a little calmer but nothing would have induced me to go back up that hill, not then nor ever after.

"After a minute or two Jano came and laid a hand on my shoulder. He was trying to reassure me, like you reassure a frightened animal. I looked up at him and he seemed a thousand miles away, on an island where the thing I had just seen had never happened. At last I managed to speak and I entreated him in God's name to tell me about the church on the Calvary hill. I could not bring myself to describe all that I had seen, but I told him I had seen *something* in the painting of the Last Judgement, and I implored him to tell me what he could about it.

"He told me that the painting was done by a local man. He had something of a name for himself locally, though I don't know whether any of his other works survive. I hope not. It seems the man had one child, a daughter, who was very beautiful. She was very graceful and slender, with very pale skin, like porcelain, and flaxen hair so blonde that it was almost white, and she liked to wear white or light colours, so that she was all white, 'like a bone,' said Jano. She was in love with a young man who lived locally, and they were engaged to be married. Then it seemed that another man, a visitor, not someone from the village, came to Tajov and fell in love with her himself. For some reason his claim superseded that of the girl's lover; either he was very much richer or he had some sort of power or hold over the girl's family. At any rate, the first engagement was broken and the girl married the newcomer. The marriage was not a success. One might not have expected perfect matrimonial harmony considering the circumstances of the marriage, but the difficulties ran deeper than that. The new husband was savagely cruel. Perhaps the knowledge that he did not have his wife's whole heart made him vicious. Well, it ended in the girl's being made away with, or dying in some terrible circumstances. The girl's father swore to have the husband's neck, whatever it cost him, and gathering some friends he went to seek him out, but the bird had flown and he was cheated of his revenge. It was believed afterwards, that the painting of the Last Judgement, which he was later commissioned to make, had his vengeance somehow painted into it. The mural was not well-received amongst the local congregation, though Jano could not say exactly why this was; it was not liked but no-one cared to paint over it, even after the painter was long dead and gone. Instead the little church fell gradually into disuse.

" 'When did all this happen?' I asked.

"Jano shrugged. 'A very long time ago.'

" 'How long? Fifty years? A hundred?'

" 'Maybe.'

" 'And is there some story attached to the church—I mean, did anything subsequently happen, anything odd?'

"Again the shrug. 'Just very unlucky.'

" 'And the girl,' I persisted. 'What was her name?'

"Jano looked away, scanning the walls and the doorway with his eyes. At last he said, 'I think it was maybe Ludmila . . . something like that.' He did not catch my eye. At last I laid a hand on his forearm and he looked at me.

" 'Jano,' I said, 'please—take me to the house.'

"I didn't need to tell him which one. He sighed very heavily as though I had asked him to do something which he really did not want to do. But at length he nodded, and we got to our feet. I went to the bar to pay for the drinks, but the barman refused to take anything for them. Either Jano had already paid or he didn't want my money. I didn't much care which. I was nearly at the end of a long and weary road and I just wanted it over with.

"We walked up through the village without speaking. It was still hot, and the road was dusty. I don't think I could ever have found the place on my own; I didn't see a single road name anywhere in Tajov, much less anything corresponding to the scrawl in Robert's notebook. We took a right-hand turning and found ourselves coming to the edge of the village. Beyond us rose the thickly-forested hills. I tried to keep track of the house numbers as we walked; when we passed 117, I started to look a little more closely. At last we came to the very last house on the left-hand side of the road. It was small, neat and of relatively recent construction. On the front wall by the door were three blue-and-white tiles reading 123.

" 'Are you sure it was 123?' I asked Jano.

"He shook his head. 'No, I am not sure. This handwriting is not good. It could say 123, it could say 125. I am not sure which. But this is 123.' He indicated the house.

"I hesitated for a moment, then laid my hand on the gate. We went up the garden path together and knocked on the door. We waited for what seemed like an age, and then at last the door was opened by a little wizened old man who stood blinking at us through thick spectacles. Jano spoke to him briefly, and he seemed about to turn and close the door on us, but Jano swiftly added something that made the old man pause. A long stream of Slovakian followed, accompanied by much head-shaking, and at last the old man gave a final nod, and went back into the house, closing the door behind him.

" 'What did he say?' I asked, almost boiling over with frustration.

" 'He says he doesn't know your brother's girlfriend,' said Jano. 'He lives there on his own. He has only two sons, no daughters, and both of them work in Bratislava. I think he is angry with them for going away.'

"I couldn't have cared less about the old man's problems with his sons. 'Well, who lived here before?' I asked.

" 'I don't think anyone,' said Jano. 'It's not that old.'

"He was right. I could feel my shoulders sagging with defeat. 'Are you sure he didn't have a daughter?' I persisted. 'What if he had one and she died?'

" 'No, definitely no daughter,' said Jano firmly. 'I asked him this in the best way I could without being rude. He has never had any daughters. Only two sons.'

"So that was it. The end of the road. I stood with my hands on my hips and scanned the scene for some inspiration, some sign to indicate where I should go next, what I should do with this trail that lead nowhere. And then my eyes lit upon the patch of ground next to number 123 where the old man had his neat little house. You know, there are some plants which especially love to grow in places where the earth has been disturbed—rose-bay willowherb is one; they sometimes call it fireweed because it grows where the ground has been burnt. Well, just on this particular patch of ground there was a whole profusion of that kind of plant. When I really looked, when my eyes and my brain had adjusted to what I was seeing, it was quite obvious: there was a big squarish patch where something had been before, where the earth had been disturbed or something had been built which now had gone. I left Jano standing outside the garden gate of number 123 and went to have a closer look. Why had I not seen it before? It was plainer and plainer the more closely I looked. I stepped carefully into the midst of the tangled plants and began to kick about with my feet, looking for stones or bricks or anything which might tell me that number 125 had once stood here. Almost at once I felt something hard underfoot. It was a roofing tile. I lifted it carefully and began to pick my way back to the road, holding it in my hand. I am not sure what I intended to do with it, or what I intended to say to Jano. And then, just as I was about to step back onto the firmer surface of the road, I felt something crunch under my shoe. I looked down, and something was winking in the evening sunlight; a piece of glass, now broken into twinkling shards. On impulse I knelt down and cleared the foliage away from it with my hand.

" 'What is it? What did you find?' called Jano. I did not answer him. I was slowly rising to my feet, with something clasped in my right hand; something which I recognised. I took a step forward and tried to hold it out to him, this thing I had found there under the weeds. Robert's spectacles—the rims spotted with rust, one of the lenses smashed to smithereens by my shoe, but still unmistakably his.

"And then at last I sank to my knees there in the dusty road, and wept; wept for the brother I had always loathed."

Story Notes

Grauer Hans

The setting of "Grauer Hans" is never explicitly identified, but I had Bad Münstereifel in mind. I lived in the town, which is not far from Cologne, for seven years, and it inspired my first novel, *The Vanishing of Katharina Linden*, as well as providing the location. Bad Münstereifel is a place with a long and colourful history (plague, floods, war, witch trials) and a great many local legends. The figure of Grauer Hans himself was inspired by a tradition that a friend in Münstereifel related to me. In Germany, as well as other European countries such as Holland and Belgium, Saint Nicholas brings presents to good little children on the eve of 6th December. He is sometimes accompanied by a less amiable figure, personified as Knecht Ruprecht or Krampus, who punishes badly-behaved children. Allegedly this character was known locally as Hans and was supposed to abduct naughty children; the friend told me that in the past when someone dressed as Saint Nicholas visited the children of the town, he would be accompanied by someone called Hans who would put the naughty ones in a sack and shake them around to give them a fright. I have not been able to verify this story but over the border in Alsace, Saint Nicholas' companion is known as Hans Trapp, so who knows? At any rate, this folk tale made an evil impression on me and largely inspired my own "Grey Hans".

Story Notes

❦

The Sea Change

"The Sea Change" came about because in my late twenties and early thirties I was a keen scuba diver. I discontinued the hobby after the arrival of our two children and our subsequent removal to a landlocked part of Germany. However, I was very keen to use my experiences to write a sub-aqua ghost story, although for a long time I was rather stumped about how to do this. Like my story's protagonist, I always found wreck-diving peculiarly creepy, especially in British waters, which are generally exceedingly murky. There are plenty of opportunities for chilling moments on wreck dives; supposing, for example, one were to be diving the wreck of a wartime submarine and one heard hammering from inside? The difficulty, however, is to make a satisfying story out of these moments. The solution came from an aspect of diving which has literally haunted me in nightmares which I still occasionally have, more than a decade after giving up: the thought of inadvertently staying down at the bottom much longer than one should. In real life this would mean a bend, or running out of air; in "The Sea Change" it means something else altogether.

❦

The Game of Bear

"The Game of Bear" is an unfinished story by the great M.R. James, which was transcribed from James's manuscript in the archive at King's College, Cambridge by Rosemary Pardoe and first published in the *M.R. James Ghosts and Scholars Newsletter 12* (2007). The *Newsletter* subsequently ran a competition to complete the story, of which mine was the winning entry. Different versions have been published by other authors including Clive Ward and Reggie Oliver.

I have been a fan of the ghost stories of M.R. James since I was a child and my father used to regale us on boring journeys by retelling them. Obviously an opportunity to collaborate with the great man himself, even at a distance of a century, was irresistible. The fragment itself runs to just over 1700 words and gives very little away; two elderly men are discussing "the Purdue business", which evidently relates to the death of a mutual friend, the circumstances of which were in some way so shocking that one of the men is no longer able to cope with sudden screams and shouts. Clearly there is some kind of grudge involved on the part of the dead man's unlikeable cousin. So far, so intriguing; but there is little to suggest how the cousin's malice translated itself into Purdue's demise, other than the fact that aspects of "The Game of Bear" recall the death in some shocking way.

For me, MRJ's most frightening inventions have a tinge of *wrongness*. The "horrible hopping creature in white" of "Casting the Runes" springs to mind: there is something so dreadfully unnatural about anything predatory that hops. I tried to give the horror at the centre of my story something of that quality.

Trying to complete a story started by MRJ is exciting but it also feels presumptuous; it is for the reader to judge whether this version is successful or not.

My completion of "The Game of Bear" is republished here by kind permission of N.J.R. James and Rosemary Pardoe.

❧

Self Catering

"Self Catering" was a bit of a departure from the norm for me, because it has a certain amount of humour as well as the pre-requisite nastiness at the end. The story is driven by the fussy, anxious and sometimes pompous character of the narrator (I won't call him hero), Larkin. As for his hearty and provoking colleague Watson—haven't we all worked with someone like that?

❧

Nathair Dhubh

"Nathair Dhubh", which was published in *All Hallows 39* in 2005, was the first of my short stories to appear in print. Although my first three novels all have female narrators, in my short fiction I sometimes fall naturally into a male narrative voice. I think of "Nathair Dhubh" as more of an "old-fashioned ghost story" than some of my other tales, because it is set between the Wars, and the voice of "Jim" seems to fit that.

Just as "The Sea Change" is set in the world of scuba diving, "Nathair Dhubh" is set in the world of rock climbing. I *have* climbed myself, but not to a very high standard. I'm fascinated by the evolution of outdoor equipment—it is always astounding to see what climbers and mountaineers wore in the '20s and '30s in comparison to the high tech equipment they have now. I liked the idea of Tom and Jim climbing in their old-fashioned boots! Also the fact that when they go off to climb Nathair Dhubh they are alone in a landscape populated only by sheep. Outdoor activities have become so much more mainstream that a popular peak may be visited by thousands or even tens of thousands of mountaineers a year. Jim's world is idyllic as well as dangerous.

∾

Alberic de Mauléon

"Alberic de Mauléon" was written as an entry for another competition in the *M.R. James Ghosts and Scholars Newsletter*, this time to write a prequel or sequel to an MRJ story. The best entries were collected in *The Ghosts and Scholars Book of Shadows*, published by Sarob Press in 2012. I had several ideas for my entry, one of them a modern sequel to "A Neighbour's Landmark", which is one of my favourite stories by M.R. James; but in the end I had to go for this one, which is (obviously) a prequel to "Canon Alberic's Scrap-book".

In 2004 I visited St. Bertrand de Comminges, where "Canon Alberic's Scrap-book" is set. I've always been inspired by real-life locations and Comminges is an exceptionally inspiring place. The visit furnished me with some of the small details that appear in my story, such as the carving of the rich man being swallowed by a demon on the cathedral doorway.

I've long been fascinated by the tale of Canon Alberic, particularly by all the unanswered questions. What, for example, was the thing that the Canon was seeking, about which he inquired on 12th December 1694? Who was it that gave him the replies to his questions? And why did he make the drawing of the creature that so terrified him? I tried to answer these questions in my story.

∾

Story Notes

The Calvary at Banská Bystrica

Of all my short stories, "The Calvary at Banská Bystrica" is probably my personal favourite. I very much enjoyed creating a story in which there is a "back story" hidden behind the narrative of the brother searching for his lost sibling. Like others of my stories, it was inspired by a real place. Some years ago we visited Slovakia with some German friends; I knew absolutely nothing about the country and probably would never have thought of going there if the other family had not proposed it. We stayed in a village quite close to Banská Bystrica and spent a lot of time in the town. It was exactly as I have depicted it in the story, even down to the wine shop, although of course "Jano" is an invention.

The Calvary hill at Tajov is a real place too. We visited it on a hot dry afternoon, just as the narrator of the story does. The path up to the church was very overgrown and we did not see or hear any other living thing apart from the insects droning. The effect was a rather insinuating stillness. When we reached the church and looked inside to see the painting of the Last Judgement (which again, is exactly as I have described it in the story), I was very odiously impressed. Before we were halfway down the hill again, I had started composing the story in my head.

Sources

My thanks to the following editors and publishers
for the first appearance of these stories, as follows:

"Grauer Hans"
was first published in *Shades of Darkness*,
edited by Barbara Roden & Christopher Roden.
Ash-Tree Press, October 2008.

"The Sea Change"
was first published in *Supernatural Tales #11*,
edited by David Longhorn, Winter 2007.

"The Game of Bear"
was first published in *The Ghosts & Scholars
M.R. James Newsletter #12*, September 2007,
edited by Rosemary Pardoe.

"Self Catering"
was first published in *All Hallows #43*,
edited by Barbara Roden & Christopher Roden.
Ash-Tree Press, Summer 2007.

"Nathair Dhubh"
was first published in *All Hallows #39*,
edited by Barbara Roden & Christopher Roden.
Ash-Tree Press, June 2005.

Sources

"Alberic de Mauléon"
was first published in *The Ghosts & Scholars
Book of Shadows*, edited by Rosemary Pardoe.
Sarob Press, October 2012.

"The Calvary at Banská Bystrica"
was first published in *At Ease with the Dead*,
edited by Barbara Roden & Christopher Roden.
Ash-Tree Press, June 2007.

About the Author

Helen Grant has a passion for the Gothic and for ghost stories. Joyce Carol Oates has described her as "a brilliant chronicler of the uncanny as only those who dwell in places of dripping, graylit beauty can be". A lifelong fan of the ghost story writer M. R. James, Grant has spoken at two M. R. James conferences and appeared at the Dublin Ghost Story Festival. She lives in Perthshire with her family, and when not writing, she likes to explore abandoned country houses and swim in freezing lochs. Her novels include *Ghost* (2018) and *Too Near the Dead* (2021).

SWAN RIVER PRESS

Founded in 2003, Swan River Press is an independent publishing company, based in Dublin, Ireland, dedicated to gothic, supernatural, and fantastic literature. We specialise in limited edition hardbacks, publishing fiction from around the world with an emphasis on Ireland's contributions to the genre.

www.swanriverpress.ie

"Handsome, beautifully made volumes . . .
altogether irresistible."

– Michael Dirda, *Washington Post*

"It [is] often down to small, independent, specialist presses
to keep the candle of horror fiction flickering . . . "

– Darryl Jones, *Irish Times*

"Swan River Press has emerged as one of the most inspiring
new presses over the past decade. Not only are the books
beautifully presented and professionally produced, but they
aspire consistently to high literary quality and originality,
ranging from current writers of supernatural/weird fiction
to rare or forgotten works by departed authors."

– Peter Bell, *Ghosts & Scholars*

GHOSTS

R. B. Russell

Ghosts contains R. B. Russell's debut publications, *Putting the Pieces in Place* and *Bloody Baudelaire*. Enigmatic and enticing, they combine a respect for the great tradition of supernatural fiction, with a chilling contemporary European resonance. With original and compelling narratives, Russell's stories offer the reader insights into the more hidden, often puzzling, impulses of human nature, with all its uncertainty and intrigue. There are few conventional shocks or horrors on display, but you are likely to come away with the feeling that there has been a subtle and unsettling shift in your understanding of the way things are. This book is a disquieting journey through twilight regions of love, loss, memory and ghosts. This volume contains "In Hiding", which was shortlisted for the 2010 World Fantasy Awards.

> *"Russell's stories are captivating for their*
> *depth of mystery and haunting melancholy."*

– Thomas Ligotti

> *"Russell deals in possibilities beyond the rational."*

– Rue Morgue

> *"Quiet horror told in an unassuming,*
> *polished narrative style."*

– Hellnotes

YOU'LL KNOW WHEN YOU GET THERE

Lynda E. Rucker

A woman returns home to revisit an encounter with the numinous; couples take up residence in houses full of sinister secrets; a man fleeing a failed marriage discovers something ancient and unknowable in rural Ireland . . .

In her introduction, Lisa Tuttle observes that "certain places are doomed, dangerous in some inexplicable, metaphysical way", and the characters in these stories all seem drawn in their own ways to just such places, whether trying to return home or endeavouring to get as far from life as possible. These nine stories by Shirley Jackson Award winner Lynda E. Rucker tell tales of those lost and searching, often for something they cannot name, and encountering along the way the uncanny embedded in the everyday world.

"Indirection is a special skill and it's one that Lynda E. Rucker uses frequently to emphasise those near indefinable moments of social alienation and paranoia, that you just want to get up and run far, far away from."

– Adam L. G. Nevill

"Lynda is the genuine article—a serious, literary author of 'quiet horror' whose work is disquieting, inspiring, and oddly reassuring. It's good to know that there are writers so gifted working in our genre."

– *Supernatural Tales*

STRANGE EPIPHANIES

Peter Bell

A mentally disturbed woman is entrapped in Beltane rituals in the Cumbrian fells; a widower mourning his wife falls beneath the mystic allure of Iona; a quest to the Italian Apennines brings a lonely man to a dread Marian revelation; an alcoholic on a Scottish isle is haunted by a deceased chronicler of local legend; in a small German town a sinister doll discloses truths about a murky family tragedy; an unknown journal by a Victorian travel-writer sends a woman on a grim odyssey to Transylvania; in a childhood holiday paradise a man encounters a demented artist's terrifying legacy. The protagonists in Peter Bell's stories confront the awesome, the numinous, the uncanny, the lure of genius loci, and landscapes undergoing strange epiphanies.

"Bell is not a purveyor of pure horror, but of something much more interesting . . . Bell's world is shot through with strange beauty but full of tragic and alarming occurrences."

– Wormwood

"A Dazzling Collection of Weird Fiction Gems . . . All the stories in Strange Epiphanies are virtually pitch perfect."

– Dead Reckonings